The Barons of Texas: Jill

FAYRENE PRESTON

Published by Silhouette Books
America's Publisher of Contemporary Romance

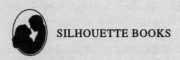 SILHOUETTE BOOKS

ISBN 0-373-76288-7

THE BARONS OF TEXAS: JILL

Copyright © 2000 by Fayrene Preston

Books by Fayrene Preston

Silhouette Desire

The Barons of Texas: Tess #1240
The Barons of Texas: Jill #1288

*The Barons of Texas

FAYRENE PRESTON

published her first book in 1981 and has been publishing steadily ever since. This is her second novel for Silhouette Books, and she is delighted to be on board. Fayrene lives in north Texas and is the mother of two grown sons. She claims her greatest achievement in life is turning out two wonderful human beings. She is also proud to announce the arrival of her first grandchild: a beautiful baby girl. Now she has even more to be thankful for.

IT'S OUR 20th ANNIVERSARY!
We'll be celebrating all year,
Continuing with these fabulous titles,
On sale in April 2000.

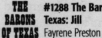

One

Jill Baron came to an abrupt halt. Her backyard was spinning around her. Slowly she took a deep breath and waited, knowing, hoping, logic would soon reassert itself. She'd owned her North Dallas home for the past ten years, and not once had its grounds ever moved, much less spun.

In fact, not one acre of Texas's vast land had ever moved. Sandstorms could whip large amounts of West Texas sandy topsoil through the air. Tornados could lift entire houses, trees and cars. But the ground always stayed still. She took comfort in the thought, and soon her backyard came to a stop.

There…there. Everything was going to be just fine.

"Can I do anything for you before I leave?"

Jill flinched. She'd thought she was alone. She turned and made an effort to smile at her executive assistant. "Not a thing, Molly."

"Are you sure? You're looking pale."

"Everyone looks pale at night." She valued Molly for her quiet efficiency and organizational ability, but Molly occasionally showed the regrettable tendency to try to mother her. She hadn't had a mother since she was three years old, and she certainly didn't need or want one now.

"You never look pale, Jill. Listen, I can run upstairs and bring down your medicine."

"*No.*" She briefly closed her eyes. "I'm sorry. I didn't mean to be so abrupt, but you know how I feel about that stuff. Anyway, I'm fine, and you've worked hard today. The party went extremely well. Thank you for your part in that. Now go home and get some sleep."

"If you're sure?" Molly still looked concerned.

"I am."

"Then I'll see you in the morning."

"Good night." Jill sipped again from the champagne bottle she carried, then stared down into the pool. Blue filters over its lights had created a lovely pale-blue oasis of breeze-rippled water with lotus-blossom-shaped candles floating on its surface.

Her eyes narrowed. Bright. The flames were too bright. She poured champagne onto one of the candles, dousing its flame. Resuming her walk along the edge of the pool, she continued pouring until every candle flame was out, then drank more champagne.

She wasn't yet ready to go into the house. This was her favorite time of any party she gave. The last of her guests had gone. Both the band and the caterers had finished packing up and were also gone. She liked reclaiming her home and its grounds. She liked the return of the quiet and the order. But more than that, she liked the feeling of accomplishment she felt after a really successful party.

The pool moved. The ground beneath her shifted. She stopped and frowned down at her bare feet, which peeked out from beneath the hem of her cream-colored designer gown. The ground wasn't moving. Neither was she. *Damn.*

Perhaps she'd had more champagne than she had realized, but just as fast as the thought occurred, she dismissed the idea. She'd never been drunk in her life, plus she rarely drank at her parties until the last guest had left. She didn't like to give up control of anything, much less her mental faculties. She waited, and after several moments her patience was rewarded when everything stilled once again.

With a mental shrug, she took another sip of champagne. It was going to be okay.

The party had been extremely productive. She had been able to bring Holland Mathis to the point that one more visit with him would have him signing on the dotted line for those three buildings in the southeast corner of downtown Dallas she'd been trying to get for so long. She'd even been able to get Tyler Forster interested in renovating the buildings into residential condominiums. All in all, things had gone very well.

Her business was booming. She should feel more than satisfied at all she was accomplishing. And she was.

Except…

The lit pool had an odd aura around it, she noticed, as if the blue lights had risen into the air to form a shimmering, transparent cloud. Shimmering, transparent cloud? That made *no* sense at all.

Mind over matter, she told herself firmly. She refused to give in to this. She couldn't, *wouldn't,* let it happen again. She turned her back to the pool and strolled to a grassy area, where a border of red geraniums backed by white spring bells bloomed. The grass felt soft and cool to her bare feet. Yes, this was much better.

Sipping at the champagne, she determinedly returned to her original train of thought, which was the feeling of fulfillment at all she was accomplishing. Her achievements were a source of great gratification to her.

Yet…there was something missing.

All her life, she'd set goals and met them. This was the year that, according to her father's will, if she was able to meet a certain financial criterion set by him, she would inherit one-sixth of the family company. But she'd met that goal several years ago, and her business was going better than it ever had. So what could possibly be missing?

She came to a dead stop. *Des.* Of course. *Des!*

To date, winning her stepcousin's agreement to marriage was the only goal she had not been able to attain.

"What's the matter? Couldn't find a glass?"

Startled, Jill whirled around, in the process almost losing her balance. *"Colin."*

Colin Wynne smiled lazily and reached for the champagne. "If you're going to drink from the bottle, this is the way you should do it." He tilted his head back and downed the remaining champagne in a matter of seconds.

"I don't need lessons in drinking champagne." She snatched the bottle back from him.

"No, you don't, which is why it's so interesting to see you drinking straight from the bottle. I've never seen you do that before. Come to think of it, I've never seen you barefoot before, either. Pale pink toenails—not a very strong statement, Jill."

He was talking uncharacteristically loudly, she thought. It was almost as if she was hearing his words in Sensurround sound. "I wasn't trying to make a statement."

"That's good, because you didn't." He shrugged in a way that clearly indicated he couldn't be held accountable for her bad taste, goading her as he so frequently did, pushing her buttons until she lashed back.

"There are a great many things you haven't seen me do before, but that doesn't mean any of them are interesting or, for that matter, that you'll ever see me do them."

"Ah, but that's where you're wrong."

"Wrong?" She pressed her fingers to a spot above her right temple. He was confusing her. Of all her acquaintances, why did it have to be *Colin* who had returned? They moved in the same charity and social circle, but lately that circle seemed to be getting smaller and smaller, until every time she turned around, Colin was there. Tonight, though, she had only herself to blame, since she had included him on her guest list.

"Everything you do interests me, Jill. Where are your shoes?"

He still wasn't making any sense. And now that he mentioned it, where *were* her shoes, and why did he care? "What are you doing here? I thought I saw you leave."

A memory flashed through her head of Colin escorting an attractive young woman around the side of the house toward the front and the driveway. She remembered thinking that the woman's red hair had clashed violently with the unfortunate orange dress she'd chosen to wear. "You *did* leave. You left with Corine."

"I drove her home, which is exactly three blocks from here, as you know, then returned to wait out front until all the guests had left."

She frowned. "For heaven's sake, why?"

"Why did I take Corine home? Because the people she'd come with weren't ready to leave, and she was."

"I meant, why did you come back here?"

"To check on you."

"To check...?" Stunned, she barely managed to keep her footing when the ground starting whirling around her again. She closed her eyes, willing the ground to be still. This was *not* happening. It couldn't be. She would not allow it, most *especially* in front of Colin. When the ground stabilized beneath her, she opened her eyes and saw a thoughtfulness and concern in his regard that completely unnerved her.

But then, *he* unnerved her. On some level, and in some shape, form or fashion, he always had. As usual, he looked annoyingly handsome and self-confident, with his golden skin that constantly looked as if he had just returned from a vacation in some terribly exotic, sunny locale, and his golden-brown hair that never seemed combed. Every time she looked at him, she had to fight an incomprehensible impulse to finger-comb his hair into tidiness.

And then there was that dimple in his left cheek.

Even a half smile from him could bring it into play. She had seen grown, stone-cold-sober women become totally mesmerized by it, to the point that they would forget what they'd been saying or even where they were.

As for his eyes, they were brown with golden streaks that radiated outward to create a star formation. Those eyes... She'd seen him flirt outrageously, until the woman caught in his sights was pink with delight and quiveringly ready for whatever he had in mind. It was absolutely disgusting.

But the very worst was the way he treated her. No one teased her. No one except Colin, that was. Plus, often in the middle of a party or a meeting, she would turn to find him watching her with laughter in his gaze, as if he knew a joke she didn't. On other occasions, she would get the strangest feeling that he knew *exactly* what she was thinking and why.

But now his gaze was solemn and unwavering as he looked at her. She tried to remember what she'd been about to say and couldn't. "What did you just say?"

"That I came back to check on you."

"That's right. I knew that." She took a deep breath. "What I meant to ask is *why* you came back to see..." once again, she touched her forehead "...I mean, to *check* on me?"

"Toward the end of the party, I sensed something was wrong with you, or bothering you. I thought I'd come back to see if there was something I could do to help."

She let the champagne bottle slip to the grass, not trusting herself to bend down in case the ground chose that particular moment to move again. It was like she was tipsy, except she knew she wasn't. Maybe it was simply that her blood sugar was a little low. She should have eaten more at the party. "You could have saved yourself the trouble, Colin. Nothing was or is wrong."

"No?"

"No, of course not."

When she'd first met Colin a couple of years ago at a charity function, he had shown definite interest in her, but when she hadn't returned the interest, he'd immediately backed off. Since then, she only saw him in groups. They had mutual friends and business associates, and their shared circles were made up of people just like them—high-energy, high-achieving men and women of approximately the same age.

She knew he watched her, though she couldn't understand why. But even stranger, she often found herself watching him. He could actually be quite funny, charming and interesting at times. But most often, he disconcerted or annoyed her. Like now.

She had no idea how he'd known there was something wrong when even *she* hadn't. And she had no idea what to do with him now that he was there. She frowned. No, that was wrong. She *did* know. She had to get rid of him as soon as possible.

"Look, Colin, it was very kind of you to return to check on me, but I assure you, it wasn't necessary. In fact, I was just about to go, uh..." She glanced toward her house, but couldn't think of the word, so she simply pointed. Oh, no. She silently groaned. Words were deserting her—definitely a bad sign.

Planting one careful foot in front of the other, she started walking toward the house. He fell into step beside her, and before she knew it, his warm hand slipped beneath her elbow as if to steady her. The last thing she wanted was his help or for him to guess what was wrong.

Up ahead, the path forked. Left led to the house, which wasn't that far now. She was convinced she could make it with no problem. Right led around the side of the house to the front, where Colin's car was no doubt parked. That was the path he needed to take.

"You're going inside to do what? Work?"

She started to tell him it was none of his business what she was about to do. But if she did, he was bound to make one of his barbed remarks that would leave her no choice but to answer, and she really wasn't up to it. "It's been a long day. I'll probably just go to bed."

"Pity."

Startled, she glanced around. "Excuse me?"

"It's a pity that such a beautiful woman as you is about to go to bed alone."

She stumbled. His hand on her elbow tightened to steady her. Damn the man. He never did or said what she expected. And she wanted his hand *off* her elbow.

"Unless, of course, you've got Des trapped up there in your bedroom and I don't know it."

There. He'd done it again, gotten to her with one of his barbed remarks. She jerked away from him, freeing herself from his grasp, and glared at him. "You know…you know nothing about Des."

"Ah, that's where you're wrong. I know a great deal about Des. He's become a very good friend of mine. I also know he's dead wrong for you."

"You…" She couldn't think of a single thing to say. Plus, she realized, she could no longer see

Colin's entire face. There was a blank spot covering part of it. Her field of vision was narrowing.

She couldn't deny it any longer. She was in trouble. What was more, in only a few minutes, it was going to get worse.

"Go home, Colin. *Now. Good night.*" She hurried her pace to try to get away from him, but her legs didn't seem to work right, and she miscalculated a step. This time she would have fallen if he hadn't caught her.

"Something *is* wrong," he said grimly, the loud volume of his voice beating against her in a way that was beyond excruciating. "What is it?"

She gritted her teeth. All she had to do was make it to her bedroom. "Leave me *alone.* I—"

He swept her into his arms and headed toward the back terrace. She couldn't protest anymore. Piercing pain had struck one-half of her head. She closed her eyes and tried to relax against him, but he was walking too fast. The movement felt violent. Nausea threatened. When she felt him step over the threshold into her house, she managed to open her eyes a slit.

"Just put me down here," she whispered.

He didn't answer. "Is your bedroom up or down?"

"Please—"

"Never mind." Apparently guessing, he took the stairs to the second story two at a time.

She moaned. "Please…slow down."

"What in the hell is wrong with you?" he muttered, but he did as she said. "I'm calling 911 as soon as I get you on your bed."

"No. Pharmacy…in the drawer."

"Pharmacy? You want me to call the pharmacy?"

"No. I mean…medicine."

"There's medicine in the drawer? Is that what you're saying?"

She whimpered. "Don't yell."

"Honey, you've never heard me talk as softly as I am right now. You've also never known me to be as worried as I am at this exact moment."

Worried. He was worried about her. She didn't want that, but she couldn't think of a thing to say to get him to go away.

With her eyes still closed, she sensed when they passed through the double doors of her bedroom. There, with a gentleness she wouldn't have thought him capable of, he laid her on the bed and adjusted one of the pillows behind her head. Without further discussion, he switched on her bedside lamp and opened the drawer of the nightstand. He cursed beneath his breath.

She knew what he'd seen, but she no longer had any control over the situation. Tears were stinging at the back of her eyes. The light was piercing her skull. She blindly reached out for a pillow and pulled it over her eyes.

She heard him stride into her bathroom, heard water running; then, after several moments, the mattress shifted with his weight as he sat down beside her.

"Jill, honey? Can you open your eyes? You need to look at me for a second."

It was the last thing she wanted to do. The light was going to be intolerable. She dragged the pillow off her face and slowly opened her eyes. With each hand, Colin held up six pill bottles by their tops.

"Which do you need?"

She pointed to one.

"How many?"

She held up one finger.

He lifted her head and slid his arm behind her shoulders to brace her. She took the pill with a gulp of water from the glass he offered.

She settled back onto the pillow, her eyes once again closed. ''The light…'' The lamp was turned off before she could finish the sentence. The only other light came from a low-wattage lamp in her bathroom. She tended to leave that one on all the time, which was good, because once he left, it would be safer for her if she had some light, in case she decided she needed more medication or had to go to the bathroom. ''Thank you. You can leave now. I'll be fine.'' If the pain didn't let up soon, she was going to have to try something else.

''I'm glad you're going to be fine, but in the meantime, I think I should call your doctor.''

Even with pain pounding in her head, she could appreciate the texture of his voice—low-pitched and husky with concern. ''No.''

''Jill, I'm not blind. You're in severe pain. Your doctor should know.''

''He knows.''

She heard him exhale a long breath. ''Okay, if I see that you're feeling better within the next thirty minutes, I'll hold off calling him for now. But I *am* staying with you.''

''No.'' She would never be able to relax with him there.

''Shh. Don't try to argue with me, because you won't win. Besides, it's clearly too much of an effort for you.''

He was right about that. Then, though any movement was going to be hard, she managed to roll her head slightly on the pillow and tried to reach the hairpins that had her hair bound so tightly into its French twist. Her movement brought a wave of nausea with it, and she faltered.

He gently brushed her hand aside and did it himself. When all the pins were out, he slowly, tenderly combed his fingers through her hair until it was loose and her scalp didn't feel quite as tight. Then he took her hand in his and softly stroked her forearm. She wouldn't have thought it possible, but surprisingly, his touch soothed. Normally she didn't like to be touched.

She tried to calculate the consequences of Colin's having seen her at her most vulnerable, but no thoughts could form when there was so much pain, pain that was exhausting her as she tried to fight it. So she lay very still, waiting, praying for the medicine to kick in.

"What about your dress?" she heard him ask. "Would you be more comfortable in something else?"

Yes, she would, but she simply wasn't up to changing. "Not now."

"Let me know when you think you can move without so much pain."

She attempted to blank her mind, but she was too aware of the pain, too aware of the man stroking her arm.

Colin carefully watched her, trying to think of what else he could do for her. He had recognized a couple of the names on the prescription bottles. It was medicine used for migraine headaches. Several people he knew had them. How long, he wondered, had Jill been suffering from them?

From what he'd heard about migraines, she was a prime candidate for them—type A personality, a perfectionist through and through who worked extremely hard.

Tonight had been a perfect example. She hadn't enjoyed the party. She had *worked* the party. And he knew her well enough to know that his invitation, along with many others, had been extended to make up the numbers she needed. There had really been only two or three people she had wanted to talk to, though she was a professional at camouflaging her intent.

His eyes traveled down her body. For the party, she had worn a high-necked, narrow column of ivory silk crepe that discreetly skimmed her body, leaving only her arms bare. It was a dress in perfect taste, yet on her, it had a subtle sexiness to it that was enough to bring a man—hell, *him*—to the point where he was almost ready to beg to see more. But he knew that was no way to get to Jill, so he had forced himself to stay away from her and merely watch.

From the first moment he'd met her, something about her had gotten to him. She was a classically, breathtakingly beautiful woman, with her sleek dark hair and lovely bourbon-colored eyes. They had both been attending a glittering affair in a gilded ballroom with tall candles, the room filled with women draped in jewels and shimmering gowns. But to him, Jill had stood out among the peacocks. She'd worn no jewels, only the unadorned elegance of a slim, strapless, red velvet gown. He could still remember how her skin had glowed in the candlelight.

Right off the bat, she'd rebuffed him in a manner that had been almost automatic. He'd been amused. Rebuffing men was obviously instinctive with her, and because of it, he'd been challenged.

At first his attraction had been simple and basic— a burning, hungry, primal need that made him want to grab her, take her to the nearest place where they could be alone and have sex with her until they were both too spent and tired to do anything but go to sleep.

He had watched her for the rest of that evening, and as he did, there had been a moment when she had turned away from someone she'd been talking with. In that instant, he'd seen something that had connected with him on his deepest, most elemental level. In that moment, he had recognized a depth in her that held much more than what she allowed the world to see. Still, he wasn't certain what it was about her that he had connected with so strongly. Only later, after other encounters, had he figured it out.

Loss and need.

He had seen scars of loss in her, wounds not entirely healed and hurts remembered as if they had happened yesterday. He had recognized that in her because he had some of the same things in him, maybe not as deep, maybe not as hurtful, but he definitely knew what loss and need were all about. Their experiences might have been different, but the pain was the same.

The knowledge made him realize that the wait for her to turn and look at him as a desirable man whom she wanted in her life would be well worth the patience that would be required. The knowledge also made him more determined than ever to have her, because he knew that, deep inside, where all the holes and hurt were, they could help each other.

It hadn't taken him long to learn she was interested in only one man. Des Baron. Once he'd figured out the whys and wherefores, he had known she and Des wouldn't work out. The bone-deep certainty had come from knowing that *he* was the only man she should ever be with, and that sooner or later he was going to make her his. What he hadn't known was how long it would take him. Luckily, he had plenty of patience.

He had made it his business to study her, learn her moods—what made her happy, what made her unhappy. It hadn't been easy. Jill, by her own design, had built a formidable barrier around herself. Only recently had he begun to see cracks in her barrier—small cracks, true, but for Jill, even a tiny splinter fracture was extraordinary.

Maybe the ongoing problem of the migraines had been the cause of the cracks. Or perhaps she was simply running out of challenges, something he knew, because he had made it a priority to know every move she made, business, as well as personal. And because of it, could almost guarantee he knew what was coming next. It was what he'd been waiting for.

But tonight, as the party had continued, he'd noticed that her eyes had taken on a bruised look, something someone who knew her only on a social or a business level wouldn't have noticed. But he had, and it was the reason he had returned.

"How are you doing?" he asked, his voice barely above a whisper. "Do you feel like putting on something else now?"

A shudder racked her body. "I'm cold."

Before she could say anything more, he was up and

walking into her closet. He dismissed the rows of perfectly hung business suits, dresses, blouses and skirts, and zeroed in on a full-length beige knit nightgown with long sleeves and a matching robe. His hand closed over the knit. It was a cashmere blend. Perfect. Someone in pain should be encased in softness.

Beside her again, he saw that her eyes were open. He tossed the matching robe on the end of the bed. "Is this okay?" He held up the gown.

She gave an ever-so-slight nod, then closed her eyes once more. "I can do it."

It made sense that, under any circumstances, she would be adamantly opposed to having him help her change her clothes, but tonight her formidable determination to control all things involving herself was vastly diminished, and as weak as she appeared, she wouldn't be able to change her clothes without help.

He had to divert her attention, and he had the perfect topic. "I know you can," he murmured casually, "but as long as I'm here, I might as well make myself useful."

With the greatest of care, he raised her to a sitting position. He had pitched his voice so low he wasn't certain she could hear him, but there was one statement he knew would probably raise her from the dead. "Besides, there's something I need to tell you—well, really it's a confession, and it's this. I know you'll agree with me when I say how seldom I'm wrong." She made a faint sound of disgust. He smiled. She could hear him. Good. "Well, as it turns out, I was wrong tonight. You don't have Des up here, after all."

"Des didn't...come."

"He never comes to your parties, does he?"

"Some."

"Anyone would think he didn't like you." He quickly slid the zipper down to below her waist, then slipped the dress off her arms.

"He likes…"

The lined dress fell to her waist. He paused, and his throat went dry when he saw the cream-colored, sheer lacy bra she was wearing. He brought her forward to lean against him so that he could reach around her and undo the bra. Perfume rose from her skin as the bra fell away to reveal rose-colored areolas and tight pointed nipples. He felt himself harden, and his mouth began to water.

He tossed the bra toward the closet and forced himself to continue. "I'm guessing that you've decided now is the time to pull out all the stops and go after him, am I right?" He slipped the sleeveless knit gown over her head. "Raise your arms for me."

"No." There was a lack of comprehension in her bruised eyes, but he sensed she was trying hard to focus on what he was saying. "Des likes me."

"Yes, he does—as a member of his family. Lift your arms, honey, so I can put on the gown." Slowly she did. "But I feel I should tell you that you don't have a chance in hell of getting him into bed, much less to the altar."

"No. I do. I mean, why…why would you think I don't?"

He forced himself to concentrate on getting her arms through the openings of the gown's sleeves and not looking at her breasts. Still, the back of his hand brushed the top of one of them, causing his breath to catch in his throat. He almost groaned. Her breasts were exactly as he had imagined them to be—high, round and firm, large enough to fill his hands, but not large enough to make a man's neck whip around when she walked by. Just as he liked, wanted.

"Well, first of all," he said, the huskiness in his voice revealing the effect she was having on him, "as I said before, he considers you family, and I can't see you changing his mind on that. After all, you're not exactly a femme fatale, now are you?"

"I am..."

He pulled the gown down over her breasts, thankful that he had finished that part of undressing her. It had to be the most difficult part. At least, he hoped it would be. He didn't know how much temptation he could stand. "You are what?"

"A femme..."

"Fatale?" he supplied when she couldn't seem to come up with the last word.

"Yes." She looked down at the gown that covered her to her waist as if she'd didn't have a clue how it had gotten there.

"Lie back down." He cradled her head in his palm and eased her back to the pillow and bed. "As for you being a femme fatale, I would really like to agree with you, but I'm afraid I can't." An out-and-out lie, but now was not the time to profess how easily she could make him want her. Even a gesture as simple as lifting a canape to her mouth could have him fighting to resist vaulting the table and kissing her until all her barriers were down and she didn't care where she was or who was watching.

He stood, bent over her and eased the rest of the ivory sheath over her hips, down her legs and off. For a minute he just stared. She was wearing a tiny scrap of silk and lace that matched her bra.

"I'm going to have Des eating out of my…"

"Hand?" Once again he supplied the word she couldn't seem to come up with, but his voice was rough with the desire that was rising in him, too fast, too uncontrolled. He had to be careful. As out of it as she was, she still might begin to notice.

"I need him."

He cleared his throat. "The problem is, you say you need him, but you don't. It's a matter of what you *want*—you *want* the fifty percent of Baron International Des will inherit from your uncle William when William dies, so that you can screw your sisters to the wall with your majority holding." He forced himself to toss the panties toward the bra and pull the gown down as much as he could.

"Yes. No." She pressed her hand to a spot above her right temple. "When we marry, I'll gain his fifty percent of…our, uh…business. Company."

"That's what I just said."

She remained silent, obviously trying to figure out the conversation.

"Are you that anxious for your uncle William to die?"

Her eyes flew open, then quickly closed again. "No. I love him."

"Sometimes I wonder if you even know how to love," he muttered. "No one would think so if they heard your plan."

"What?"

"Nothing. Sit up again." As before, he helped her up. She was like a limp doll, her body working only because of his strength. He pulled the top covers from beneath her and slid her pillow back into position as he slowly returned her head to its softness. He couldn't tell whether she was feeling less pain or not. "Besides, strictly speaking, *you* won't gain the fifty percent, Des will, and who knows what he'll want to do with it."

"Once we're married..."

"*If* you marry him, you mean. But for argument's sake, let's say you do get him to marry you. Do you honestly think he's going to be so overwhelmed by your feminine charms that he'll just hand over his percentage?"

"Yes, he—"

"Think again, honey. Besides, do you really think you're the only woman who wants Des? And not for his future percentage of Baron International, either."

"Who?"

Now it was a fairly easy task to pull her gown over her hips down to her ankles, straighten it, then draw the covers from beneath her legs, up and over her.

"Is that better? Do you feel warmer now?"

She gave a small sigh, and he hoped the sigh meant she felt at least a bit more comfortable.

After a moment, she frowned. "Des will..." Once again she pressed her hand to the same spot she had before, the spot above her right temple. "He's never shown interest..."

"You're right. He's never shown any interest in Baron International, but I wouldn't bet against him once he inherits his father's portion. In case you don't know it, Des is a very astute businessman. How are you feeling now?"

"I..." She stopped, and he had the feeling she was having to evaluate the pain, which meant he'd been somewhat successful in preoccupying her.

"It's still bad."

He checked his watch. "It's been fifteen minutes since I gave you your medication. Should you be feeling less pain by now?"

"I will."

"You mean you'll feel better soon?"

She didn't respond. Looking down at her beautiful pale face, he felt more helpless than he could ever remember. "I'm going to call your doctor. Where's the number?"

She moaned and made an attempt to move that was quickly ended. "Sniffer."

"What?"

She lifted a shaky hand and pointed to the nightstand. "Sniffer."

He jerked the drawer open, causing pill bottles to roll every which way. "Sniffer?" Then he saw it. An inhaler. He held it up. "Is this what you want?"

She stretched out her hand for it, and he gave it to her. With his help, she struggled up to one elbow, then looked at him. "This will...put me out and I'll...be fine."

"Okay."

"Will you...go?"

"As soon as I know you're okay, I'll go."

One puff from the inhaler and she fell back onto the pillow.

He watched her for several minutes. She lay very still, though it seemed to him that she was starting to breathe easier. She had no way of knowing it, but he had zero intention of leaving her alone tonight in this big house. Anything could happen, and she wouldn't be able to help herself. "Jill?"

She didn't answer. He slid off the bed. Immediately her eyes flew open.

"Do you have to...go just yet?"

"No."

"Just a...little longer."

He could barely believe she was actually asking him to stay. For her to ask, she must be in a kind of hell he could only imagine. "Of course I'll stay, for as long as you want me to."

Her eyes closed again. "Only a...little..." Her words trailed off.

He shrugged out of his jacket, slid his tie from around his neck, rolled up his sleeves and slipped off his shoes. He eased himself down on the other side of the bed. Taking a couple of pillows, he arranged them to his satisfaction, then settled back.

She moaned, and in her drugged sleep, she edged closer to him. She must still be cold. Slowly he drew her against him, though he was on top of the covers and she was beneath them. He put his arm around her and rested her head on his chest.

For so long he'd wanted to hold her, but not like this. All he could think of was how to get her more comfortable. Again she moaned. What could he do?

Two

Something disturbed her. A scent invaded her senses. Something was happening that she didn't want to happen. Unwillingly, Jill felt herself being drawn upward through layers of blissful sleep to wakefulness, but she resisted moving or opening her eyes. Instinct told her something was wrong. She was warm and comfortable, but she felt…fragile. *Extremely* fragile.

Then she remembered. She'd had a migraine last night. It was gone, but as always, her head retained the memory of the pain. She softly sighed. She hadn't had a migraine in two months and had convinced herself that she was over them. *Damn.* To make it worse, this one had been a killer, one of the worst she'd had.

What had happened? And what was it that she was smelling? And feeling?

Trying to piece together the previous night's events, she grasped at remnants of the pictures that were floating in and out of her consciousness. The party—it had gone well. Holland Mathis and Tyler Forster were to the point of agreeing to what she wanted, which had been the main purpose of the party. Yes, she remembered. And she had even been able to lay the groundwork for future projects with others.

Champagne. Blue filtered lights. Golden brown eyes. Hair that always seemed to need combing.

Colin.

Now she remembered. He had returned, showing up in her backyard after everyone had left. He had said he'd returned because he had sensed something was wrong. That had been really strange.

Sometimes Colin could be the bane of her existence. No one could get to her the way he could. When she tried to ignore him, he refused to let her. And when she tried to cut him dead by turning a cold shoulder, he would just laugh at her.

A year ago he had offered to fly her and quite a few of their friends down to Corpus Christie in his latest toy, a new plane. The occasion had been her sister Tess's birthday party, but he'd left without her. The reason? She was fifteen minutes late, and he had refused to wait. She had been furious.

Yet other times, she would find herself attracted to him. That is, until she could manage to regain control of her senses and sternly remind herself why she couldn't be attracted to Colin. *Des* was the man she planned to marry—if she could just get him to cooperate.

Still…she owed Colin. As much as she hated even to consider the idea, she definitely owed him. When the pain had hit, he had been there for her.

She liked to think she could have taken care of herself, but truthfully, she would never know, because he had stepped in and helped her. She was going to have to come up with some appropriate way to thank him. Perhaps a plant for his office.

She inwardly groaned. How should she know what was appropriate? Maybe she would just wait until she went in to work and discuss the matter with Molly. For now, her thinking was still too fuzzy.

Slowly, she opened her eyes and saw sunlight flooding her bedroom. She gave another inward groan. Normally, as soon as the sun slanted its first rays into her bedroom, she hopped out of bed, eager to attack the day. But she didn't feel all that well just yet. She felt enervated, weak, and the urge to stay in bed was strong.

However, she had tried hard never to allow herself to use the migraines as an excuse to slack off, and she wasn't going to now. When she was at work, she tried to be more aware of the signs of an oncoming migraine. There, if necessary, she would even give herself a shot that would stop the headache dead in its tracks and allow her to continue her business day. But since she had been alone last night, she'd been reluctant to rely on medication and had tried to fight the pain off by willing it away. So much for her will.

She turned her head to glance at her bedside clock. Seven-thirty. Usually she was in her office by seven. If she got up now, she could be in by eight-thirty, nine at the latest. Experimentally, she pushed herself up in bed.

''Feeling better?''

Every muscle in her body froze. *Colin.* She twisted around and gasped.

He was lying on his back, his arm behind his head, the covers at his waist giving her a breathtaking vision of his bare chest. Golden-brown hairs curled over its width and downward to disappear beneath the covers. Dear Lord, was he naked? She closed her eyes, then quickly opened them again. "What are you doing here?"

He shifted, and the bed dipped as he angled his body toward her, came up on his elbow and propped his head up with his hand just inches from her. His face was so close she could see the fine golden-brown stubble on his jaw and the gold streaks in his eyes.

"You don't remember?"

"I..." A memory floated to the forefront of her brain. She'd been reluctant for him to leave, though she couldn't actually recall asking him to stay. But that memory brought others. The pain had been so bad she'd felt a vital, essential need to hold on to him, as if his strength could keep the pain from sweeping her away. But...

Her brow creased as she prodded her memory further. "I remember you walked around the bed and got on top of the covers." And once he was on the bed beside her, his warmth had drawn her toward him. Without really knowing what she was doing, she'd cuddled against his upper body, doing her best to soak up the heat and strength of him. But she was sure the covers had been between them.

And now she recognized the scent that had invaded her sleep. The covers and the air around her were filled with the scent of spices and musk. It was the bold, sexual scent that was uniquely Colin's and was probably on the sheets where he'd slept. "I didn't expect you to stay all night. And I didn't expect you to…uh…undress.''

He pushed himself up in bed to a sitting position. The covers fell away enough that she could see the black elastic waistband of his briefs. She breathed a quiet sigh of relief. At least he wasn't totally naked.

''The truth is, I never had any intention of leaving you alone. If you hadn't said something, I had planned to wait outside the door until I thought you were asleep, then come back in.''

She blinked. ''Why?''

''I couldn't leave you alone. You were too sick, too out of it, and there are a hundred other reasons why you shouldn't have been left alone. If you'd gotten worse, or had a reaction to the medication, or if you'd needed something, I wanted to be here. Hell, what if the house had caught on fire? You would have been defenseless. No, Jill, I couldn't leave you alone.''

She had never seen his eyes as soft as they were now. She caught her bottom lip between her teeth. A moment later, she realized what she was doing. Chewing on her bottom lip was a bad trait left over from a stressful childhood. ''And, uh, what went into the decision that moved you from on top of the bed, fully dressed, to under the covers and undressed?''

He grinned. ''Even after the medicine hit you and you went out like a light, you couldn't seem to get comfortable. I decided you still might be cold, and I was right. As soon as I undressed and got beneath the covers, I pulled you against me. Almost immediately you relaxed.''

There was nothing she could say. None of what she'd done had been conscious, and therefore she couldn't explain her actions. The medication always made her feel odd, as if she might float away. She had a vague recollection of his arm around her, of being pulled against him, of at last feeling secure and, strangely, anchored to something strong.

"How long have you been awake?"

"Since the sun came up."

"Why didn't you wake me?" For the first time irritation shaded her tone.

He responded by smiling, slowly, and she found herself caught up in watching the movement of his lips, their fullness, their sensual shape. And then there was his dimple. She stared at it, vaguely fascinated.

"Manners."

"Excuse me?"

"I didn't wake you up because it wouldn't have been polite."

"Why on earth not?"

"You were all tangled up with me."

The air went out of her lungs as the feeling came back to her of her leg between his and her arm laid across his middle. Her face grew hot. She would swear she never blushed, but now she couldn't be sure, because his gaze had suddenly narrowed on her face.

"Besides, you were sleeping so well I hated to wake you."

"But when I did wake up, you...I mean, *I* was...over *here*."

He shrugged. "I'd been lying in one position all night. My muscles had started to cramp, and I needed to stretch out. I disentangled us, though I tried hard not to wake you. Sorry."

She nodded, though she had no idea why. She was

just grateful that she hadn't awakened in his arms. That would have been incredibly awkward and excruciatingly embarrassing.

"How are you feeling?" He threw back the covers and slipped off the bed. His solid black briefs fit him as if they'd been cut just for him, and he seemed as comfortable in front of her as if he paraded around her bedroom every day, nearly naked. To him it was obviously not a big deal, but then, he must have dressed and undressed many times before in other women's bedrooms.

She barely had time to absorb that strangely disturbing thought when, with his back to her, he bent over to retrieve his trousers, offering her a view of his muscled back that tapered down to a narrow waist, then continued on to the tight roundness of his buttocks. Her throat went dry. She'd known him for more than two years, yet she'd never once thought to wonder how he would look with no clothes. Now she wouldn't have to. The close fit of his briefs left very little to the imagination.

"Jill?"

"What?"

"You never answered my question. Are you feeling better?"

In what seemed like slow motion, he drew on his trousers one leg at a time, so that she could see the arresting play of his muscles beneath his skin. In the sunlight, the hair on his legs was more golden than brown and gilded his tan. When his pants were settled around his waist, she heard the swift, efficient zip of his trousers.

She felt a pang of regret. It was such a foreign feeling to her that it left her shaken and more than a

little bemused. It was only when she realized that
Colin was looking at her with an amused expression
on his face that she realized she hadn't answered him.

"Okay. I feel okay."

"Just okay?"

"I'm fine."

"Is the pain *completely* gone?"

"All but the memory."

His eyes narrowed on her. "What's wrong, Jill?"
His words were soft and filled with concern, the concern she remembered from last night.

"Nothing. It's just...I'm sorry you felt you had to
stay all night. You couldn't have been comfortable."
Not the way she'd clung to him. "Were you even
able to sleep?"

"Yes. After you calmed and I was sure you were
sleeping well, I went to sleep."

She forced a short laugh. "I guess you're accustomed to sleeping with women."

With a glance at her that she couldn't interpret, he
reached for his shirt. "How long have you suffered
from these migraines?"

She stared at his bare chest. "Not long."

He shrugged into the shirt. "Wrong answer. I got
a glance at the dates on those prescription bottles. A
few of them date back nearly a year."

She couldn't get her mind past the fact that they
had slept in the same bed. She'd never slept in the
same bed with *anyone,* and that included her sisters.
Even more disturbing, there wasn't anything platonic
about the way she and Colin had slept together. As
he had said, she'd only really been able to fall into a
truly restful sleep when she'd been tangled up with
him. Even though sex hadn't been involved, to her

way of thinking, their night together had been incredibly intimate.

To Colin, it probably wasn't that unusual. Not that she was branding him as a womanizer. From her observation, he was as likely to show up at a function without a date as he was to show up with one. Even then, he never seemed serious about any of his dates. She should know. More than once she'd been trapped by one or the other of her female acquaintances as the woman alternately salivated over him and moaned over his lack of interest.

"The migraines aren't anything to be ashamed of, Jill." He tucked his shirt into his trousers. "What has your doctor said about them? I mean, does he know what causes them?"

She slowly shook her head. "I'm perfectly healthy, if that's what you mean. I've been through numerous tests."

His expression darkened. "If all your doctor can do is write out prescriptions for you, you should see another doctor."

"I have, and he said and did the same thing." She already felt too exposed, too vulnerable to him. She didn't want him to know any more than he already did. "But I'm getting better. The last headache I had was two months ago." She pushed the covers off her, then stopped. Since she'd awakened, she'd been so focused on Colin, absorbing the fact that they had slept together and watching him as he had dressed, that she hadn't given much thought to what she was wearing. Now she realized she was wearing only a nightgown.

"Before that, how often had you been having the headaches?"

"Never mind that. How did I get this gown on?"

"I put it on you."

"Which means you took off my clothes."

He gave her one of his lazy grins, fascinating dimple included. "Don't worry. I didn't take advantage of you."

"It never crossed my mind that you did."

The fact that he'd seen her nearly naked was enough to make her want to hide under the covers until he left. Even worse, if she had slid her leg between his, it meant that her gown could have ridden up, which brought on another thought. She shifted her bottom ever so slightly.

She began to chew on her lip. She had never been as embarrassed about anything as she was about this. From now on, whenever their eyes met, they would both know that he'd practically seen her naked. The only thing she could think to do now was to try to avoid him as much as possible in the days to come. Hopefully she would soon be able to regain her composure around him. Hopefully.

"Have you ever had to use that inhalant before? It seemed pretty potent stuff."

"No." Her doctor had warned her to be standing by her bed when she used it, because it would probably knock her out. Now she knew he had been right. But he hadn't warned her what she would do if there happened to be a man in her bed. She barely stifled a groan.

"That means that last night's headache was one of your worst. I think you should call your doctor today and tell him about it."

It took a tremendous effort, but somehow she pulled herself together. "Look, I really appreciate your being here for me last night. The headache *was* a bad one. But I'm late.'' She glanced again at the clock and saw that it was already eight. She was surprised Molly hadn't called her, but since she'd known about the oncoming headache last night, she'd probably decided not to bother her. "I'm *very* late, and I need to get up and get dressed."

She slid off the bed and stood. "Before you go, though, I'd like to ask a favor."

Damn. She really hated to be beholden to anyone, especially someone who now knew more about her—and had *experienced* more of her—than even her doctors. Irrationally, she wanted to get back into bed and pull the covers over her head. But that wasn't the way she had been taught to handle things. Instead, she looked at him and saw that his gaze was fixed on her breasts. She didn't even have to glance down to know that her nipples had tightened. She folded her arms across herself.

"Colin?" She waited until his gaze was once again level with hers, and her knees went weak at the heat she saw in his eyes. She cleared her throat. "I said I'd like to ask a favor of you."

"I heard you. Ask away."

"I'd appreciate it if you would keep the information regarding my problem to yourself."

"Problem? You mean the fact that you suffer from migraines?"

"That's what I mean."

He slung his tie around his neck. "What's the matter, Jill? Are you afraid someone might actually think you've got a chink in your armor?"

As he had so many times before, he was baiting

her. But this time, she wasn't going to bite. "Will you keep the information to yourself?"

"You know, migraines shouldn't be looked at as some sort of failure on your part, or a weakness. Besides, you're not the only one who has migraines. Quite a few of our acquaintances also have them."

"How do you know?"

He shrugged. "I listen."

She took a deep breath, disgusted with herself at how easily she let him divert her. *"Will you?"*

"Of course I won't tell anyone."

"And, uh…the rest?" Once again, she caught her bottom lip between her teeth.

He lifted his jacket off a chair and, holding it with two fingers, slung it over his shoulder. "What happened between us will stay between us."

She exhaled. He hadn't made her say the words. "Thank you."

His golden-brown eyes on her, he slowly strolled toward her. Stopping in front of her, he murmured, "You're welcome. I'm just grateful you're not still in pain." Then he slowly lowered his head and pressed a kiss to her forehead. "Take it easy on yourself today." His mouth descended to her lips, where it hovered. "Take your time getting to the office."

The warmth of his breath whispered over her lips. She held her own breath as a quiver shivered through her. Was he going to kiss her?

He touched her face in a light caress. "Eat something before you leave, and drive slowly to work." He lifted his head and gazed down into her eyes. Then he smiled. "See you in a few hours." He swiveled and headed for the door.

His hand was on the doorknob before she came to

her senses. "Wait. What do you mean, you'll see me in a few hours?"

"Have you forgotten? I have an appointment with you at two." He walked out and quietly shut the door behind him.

Stunned, she sat down on the bed.

A few hours? That was all the time she was going to have to get over what had happened? She exhaled a shaky breath. Well, okay, then. Even though she had been counting on not seeing him for a while, she would have to find some way to face him this afternoon. She had never before let herself walk away from something just because it was difficult, and she wouldn't now.

If she hadn't exactly asked him to spend the night with her, she *had* asked him to stay with her a little while longer. She didn't know why she had felt she needed him, nor did she know why she had slowly slid toward him to seek his warmth. And more.

All she really knew was that she had felt strange and lost until Colin had drawn her against him and held her through the night.

Three
***

"**G**ood afternoon, Colin." Jill eyed him cautiously across the gleaming, neatly organized expanse of her mahogany desk.

"Is it?" She was trying very hard to present her usual composed and imperturbable persona, Colin reflected, but she was trying too hard. With a satisfied smile to himself, he dropped into one of the chairs in front of her desk. After last night, no matter what she said or did, he knew she would never again be able to reconstruct the barrier she had tried so hard to keep between the two of them.

"Is it what?"

"Is it a good afternoon? Are you feeling better than you did this morning?"

"Yes, I'm just fine."

"No sign of another headache?"

"No." Her jaw clenched.

He hid another smile. She was *really* regretting his part in helping her last night. Unfortunately for her, it had happened, and though she was going to try her best to get them back to the casual acquaintanceship with which she had been so comfortable these past couple of years, he had no plans to let her.

"Now that we've covered that subject," she said tersely, "let's please drop it."

"Sure, whatever you want." He took in her outfit. She'd chosen a tailored, pin-striped navy suit paired with a cream silk blouse, buttoned at her neck. A plain gold watch at her wrist was her only jewelry. The look was unusually severe, even for her. And her hair was back up in that damnable French twist she seemed so fond of, though not as tight as it had been last night. He would bet money her head was still tender from the pain she'd suffered. "I won't ask you again unless I see you looking like you did last night."

She stared at him for several moments, emotions chasing across her face too fast for him to decipher; then she broke eye contact, opened the folder in front of her and quickly scanned its contents. "Why did you even bother to schedule this meeting, Colin? I could have told you over the phone what I'm going to tell you now. I have no intention of selling you the property that's adjacent to yours."

"Why?"

She folded her hands together and rested them on the desk. "Let's not play games. You know every one of the reasons I want to keep that piece of land. Even alone, it's going to provide a big payoff once it's developed. But I have another, very strong reason for keeping the property. You flat out stole your property away from me. And *that,* Colin, is my last reason for not selling to you. It's a matter of principle.''

"Interesting. I never knew you held grudges.'' He leaned back in the chair and rested one ankle on the knee of his other leg. He was going to enjoy this. "Besides, *stole* is a pretty strong word. I did nothing illegal or, I might add, immoral.''

"That last is debatable.'' She got up and paced to the window, which offered a panoramic view of downtown Dallas, but she didn't even give herself time to register the view before she turned back to him. "I don't know how you did it, but somehow you got wind of the fact that I was going after both of those properties. I think they got your check ten minutes before I arrived with mine.''

His shrug and expression clearly indicated, *So what?* True, he did his best to keep up with what was going on in her life, but it had been sheer luck that he'd learned of her interest in the two adjoining properties mere hours after she had made her bid. Since there were no other bids higher than hers, she had assumed hers would be accepted. Moving quickly, he had called in several favors and promised more. In the end, he had topped her bid and bought one of the properties out from under her, with the hope that she would still go ahead and buy the other.

Both parcels of land were gold mines, considering their location near the proposed new sports arena. With the right development, both of their properties would help revitalize the entire area north of the arena. If she decided not to sell to him, which he was counting on, or if she didn't buy into what his real purpose was in being there today, he wouldn't have lost anything. As she had said, just one of the properties was enough to bring in, to say the least, a very nice-sized income.

What he couldn't have foreseen was the serendipitous timing of this appointment. It had given him a chance to see her just hours after she had awoken to find him in her bed, which meant that no matter what she said or did to prove the contrary, she was still off balance with him.

"Tell me something." She strolled to her taupe leather chair and rested her hands on its high back. "Why didn't you simply buy both properties? You could have so easily. Unless...unless you couldn't come up with the money for both of them at that time. Was that it?"

He knew that not having enough money was the only reason she would be able to understand, but just to needle her a little, he chose not to completely satisfy her curiosity. "That was partly it. I bought the property outright, without offering it to other investors. As to my other reasons..." He shrugged again.

Her brow creased in puzzlement, but before she could ask another question, he spoke. "Did you even consider my offer?"

"I consider all offers that cross my desk."

"It was a good, solid offer, Jill."

"I know."

"What if I increase it?"

She shook her head. "Save yourself the time."

It was the response he'd counted on, but if he hadn't tried to buy her out, she would have wondered why. If she'd taken him up on his offer, he would have lost the chance to work closely with her, which had been the whole idea behind his purchase in the first place.

After knowing and studying her and her family for about a year, he had figured out two ways he could go about making her his. What he hadn't known was when he could put his plans into action. Buying the property had been part of his first plan. Then last night, heaven had parted its clouds and a gift had fallen into his lap. As a result, he was almost certain his second plan was about to start. Content, he waited for what he knew would come next.

She leveled a steady gaze on him. "Have you reviewed *my* offer for *your* land?"

"I've reviewed it, yes."

She fidgeted with her slim gold watch band. *"Well?"*

With a regretful expression, he spread out his hands. "I'm inclined to hang on to my land."

"I see." Once again she stared at him. When she was on top of her game, she was as good as he was at masking feelings. Today, though, he could tell she was thinking about last night. Abruptly, she reached around the chair and closed the folder. "Then we're at a stalemate. There's no sense in continuing to talk about offers and counteroffers. This meeting is over."

"Not quite."

"If I'm not willing to sell and neither are you, then I don't see what else we can talk about."

"What about working together?"

Her brow crinkled. "You mean develop our properties together?"

He nodded. If she agreed, it would give him more time with her to work on his main goal, which was to change her mind about her plan to marry Des Baron. If he couldn't, the worst thing that could happen was that he would still make millions. Plus, he now had his second plan in place.

She shook her head. "I never take on a partner in any project I'm involved with. You should know that."

"I do. But I also know that, as far as I can see, that practice is not grounded in practicality." She started to say something, but he hurried on. "I know, I know. It was what your father taught you and your sisters. But think about it, Jill. With that many acres, plus a shared vision of what we want, we would be a force to be reckoned with. Besides offices and retail stores, we could add entertainment facilities and housing. And you know as well as I do that if we work in unison on the design, configuration and spacing of green belts, the city will smile benevolently on us and grant us any permit we ask for."

"I don't do things that way, Colin." She rounded the chair and sat down again.

"I think the problem is more that you don't know *how* to work with anyone else." He slowly smiled. "Come on, Jill. You're already one of the largest land barons in Texas, plus you own enormous amounts of property around the globe. It's not as if your reputation would be ruined if, just this once, you joined up with someone else. In case you haven't noticed, very few people work alone anymore. Besides, just think of the fun we'd have."

"Fun?" For several moments her gaze fastened on his smile, his lips, his dimple. Then she seemed to catch herself. "My sister Tess sold out to another oil company in her last venture and in the process lost millions. That's not going to happen to me."

"It wouldn't if we formed an alliance. In fact, it

would put us in a position to make more than we would if we worked separately. Besides, you and I both know that Tess didn't *sell out*. She made a great deal. And anyway, that was an entirely different situation from this one.'' His voice softened. ''She made that deal for love. That wouldn't be the case with us, would it?''

She frowned. ''No, of course not.''

''Well, then?''

''No, Colin.''

''You know what? I think that 'no' of yours is automatic, as so many things are with you.''

''What do you mean?''

''All I'm asking is that you not dismiss my idea out of hand. Think about it.'' He pushed himself up from the chair, leaned forward and placed the bound folder on her desk in front of her. ''This holds a few ideas I've sketched out. Study them with an open mind, and I think you'll see the benefits of working together—an *open mind* being the key. Whether you want to, though, is an entirely different matter.'' He reached out and lightly stroked his fingers down her cheek. She flinched. ''Take care,'' he murmured with a smile, then straightened and headed for the door. He walked as slowly as he could. The last thing he wanted to do was draw her suspicions. He had his hand on the doorknob when she stopped him.

''Wait. There is, uh, one more thing I'd like to talk with you about.''

He exhaled a pent-up breath, then turned with a feigned look of surprise on his face. ''Oh, yeah? What's that?''

As he moved back toward her, a dozen thoughts went through her mind. Unfortunately, they were all

about him. He was dressed casually in a shirt, slacks
and a sport jacket, which made him look wonderful.
The problem was, she now knew what he looked like
beneath his clothes, and try as she might, she couldn't
wipe away the memories.

She remembered exactly how his muscles had rippled across his back as he'd dressed and the way
those black briefs had fit him so well that she could
picture the shape of his buttocks. Then there was the
warm, safe way she'd felt when she'd awoken in his
arms. His scent, his feel...

She wiped a hand across her brow and was surprised to find she wasn't sweating. She had to be
crazy to do what she was about to do. Bringing up
anything about last night was dangerous, but in this
case...

Instead of sitting, he stood to the side of the chair
and slipped his hand into his slacks pocket. It was a
casual stance, but in his case, it was almost a stance
of power. ''What is it?''

She cleared her throat. ''I've been remembering
more about last night, and I, uh, remember you talking about Des.''

''That's right.''

Nodding her head, she fiddled with the corner edge
of the folder he'd given her. ''As I recall, you seemed
to have very definite opinions about what he likes and
doesn't like.''

''As I said last night, we've become very good
friends.''

She glanced down at the folder. ''I would never
ask you to betray a confidence of course, but I was

just wondering...has he ever said anything about me?"

"Only in the most general of terms."

"What do you mean?"

"He sometimes refers to you and your sisters as 'the girls.'"

"As if we were one entity?" Equal parts surprise and offense filled her voice. She and her sisters had never been one entity, never been so close to one another that they were like one. Their father had seen to that.

"I don't know how much you remember about our conversation, but I did tell you that he considers you family."

Lord, the task of getting Des to the altar was going to be even harder than she had anticipated. She wiped her fingers across her forehead, realized she was repeating something she had just done, then straightened and leveled her best businesslike, unblinking gaze on him. "You also said that you felt he was dead wrong for me. That was an outrageous statement to make, Colin."

"Maybe, but it is also true."

"You can't know that for sure. No one can."

"Maybe not, but I can have an opinion based on a certain amount of knowledge."

"I see." She rose from her chair and paced to the window, then back to the desk. "And that knowledge, I assume, is partly based on your belief that I'm not a femme fatale." She hated even saying the words. She'd always prided herself on the fact that she had never used her womanly wiles to get where she was today. Now she had to wonder if she even had any womanly wiles.

"You've pretty much remembered our entire conversation."

"Yeah, it's just other parts of the night that I'm having a little trouble with." She paused, picked up a pen and tapped it against her hand. "I also remember your statement that you think I've decided that now is the time to go after him."

He smiled. "I'm right, aren't I?"

She couldn't help it. Her expression turned perplexed. "How could you possibly come to that conclusion? You don't know me that well."

"I know you better than you think, so don't even bother telling me I'm wrong on that. Let's focus on the other thing I said—that you're not a femme fatale. Are you telling me I'm wrong?"

She chewed on her bottom lip, then stopped herself. But the tapping of the pen became faster. "I've never thought about it." Until now, she added to herself.

"And now that you have…?"

Now that she had, she had to admit that he was right, though she wasn't going to give him the satisfaction of telling him so. "Up to now, I haven't focused on that particular aspect of, uh…"

"Being a woman?" he supplied helpfully.

She shrugged. "I've always been a quick study. How hard can it be?" She eyed him, something, perhaps an idea, tickling at the back of her mind. "You didn't answer my question."

"That's because I can't." He smiled. "I've never been a woman."

She almost laughed at the thought. He was one of the most masculine men she'd ever known. Why hadn't she noticed it before? As soon as the question formed in her mind, the answer followed: she wore blinders that kept her from seeing anything but business. If she hadn't been born with them—and she wasn't entirely certain that she hadn't been—then her father had strapped them on her shortly thereafter. "But you're certainly around a lot of women. I mean, you seem to...*attract* women."

"What's your point?"

"I don't know." Her answer was an honest one, but she kept prodding at her mind, trying to figure it out. Whenever she was uncertain about a decision she needed to make, she usually made a list of what she knew for a fact, so that was what she did now. "You seem to know a lot about Des. And you certainly know a lot about women."

"Where did you get that second idea?"

She drew her brows together, annoyed that he'd interrupted her fragile train of thought. "I've talked to quite a few of your castoffs."

"I don't cast off women."

"They seem to think you do."

"Think about what you just said, Jill." His tone was surprisingly gentle, but his expression was uncompromising. "That can't be true."

She threw the gold pen on the desk. "Okay, okay—they're usually just disappointed that you don't get serious about them and normally don't ask them out again beyond the first or second date."

"I don't lead women on, Jill."

She sighed, sorry she had even brought up the subject. "Look, what you do with women is your business, okay?"

He stared at her with an expression that clearly said he wasn't going to let her get away with anything.

"Don't look at me like that. You *know* women only

have to look at you to start drooling over you. And if you happen to smile at them and they see that damned dimple of yours, they're suddenly planning their wedding.''

"Once again, I think you're exaggerating.''

She folded her arms across her chest. "No, actually, I'm right on that one. You seem to only want to be friends with most of them, and from what they say, you make a great friend. But that doesn't keep them from being extremely disappointed, or hoping that one day you'll look at them in a more romantic way. At any rate, why are we talking about *your* relationships with women when we started out talking about *Des* and what he thinks about me?''

"I believe you brought up the subject of my, as you put it, relationships with women.''

"I did?'' She frowned. It was what she privately termed the day-after-a-migraine syndrome. She often had trouble keeping her mind on a subject. And after last night with Colin... *Damn.*

"What's bothering you, Jill?''

She attempted to erase all thought from her mind and tried again. "Des. Des...'' The idea that had been tickling at the back of her mind suddenly came to the front, fully formed.

He shook his head. "Sorry, but you don't have a chance with him.''

"So you say.'' She eyed him warily. "Can I trust you?''

He seemed to relax, and with a smile, he sat down on the corner of her desk. "You slept in my arms last night. If you can't trust me, who *can* you trust?''

She almost groaned. "Will you please just *forget* about that?''

He chuckled. "You're kidding, right?"

Everything in her was tensed as she walked around the desk and stopped in front of him. Even though he was sitting and she was standing, their eyes were almost even. "I'm simply trying to find out if I can confide in you without you running off to Des and telling him everything I say to you."

"I would never betray you."

She got the impression his words had a deeper meaning, but perhaps it was her imagination. But there was another problem that had nothing to do with her imagination. She was standing so close to him that she could smell him, could smell the scent she had awoken to just hours before. As unobtrusively as possible, she moved a couple of feet away.

But it didn't do her any good. Last night was indelibly etched in her brain, which was odd, since half of it had been spent in severe pain and the other half in sleep. When she had time, she needed to figure that one out.

"Okay, then, see what you think about this idea. You know Des. You know women. Would you consider teaching me how to attract Des and become a—" she swallowed against a hard lump in her throat and prayed he wouldn't laugh at her "—femme fatale?"

She paced farther away from him, then turned and came back to him, unsure what she would see on his face. But to her surprise, he was eyeing her thoughtfully.

"Say I did. What would be in it for me?"

The idea was so new she hadn't considered that part, but it made sense that he would want some form of compensation. "I don't know. What would you want? Money?"

"I've got plenty of money."

"Then what?"

"Something that wouldn't cost you a dime."

"And that would be?"

"Your agreement that we work together in developing our land."

She hadn't even seen it coming. "Damn you, Colin. You know—"

"I *do* know," he said, cutting her off. "Family custom. So you're going to have to decide which is more important to you—the teachings of a father who is long dead or getting Des."

With a sound of anger, she whirled away and began pacing the conference area of her office. Comfortable chairs surrounded a long meeting table. Couches flanked a fireplace. A refreshment center was in a corner. But she barely noticed any of it. It seemed her brain would only hold Colin, and to think clearly, she had to get away from him, away from his smell that was still in her sheets at home, away from his smile that kept diverting her.

The funny thing was that she wasn't a pacer. The new habit seemed to have started since last night. Damn, she had done it again. Even the two words— last night—had the power to bring memories flooding back. As firmly as she could, she pushed those thoughts aside and tried to train her mind on the problem at hand.

Thinking rationally and adding up everything she knew to be true, she could come to no other conclusion. Colin would be an enormous help to her in her effort to gain not only Des's attention but, more importantly, his agreement to marriage.

What was more, without even looking at his ideas, she knew he was right. If they developed their properties together, they stood to make more money. It made sense. Everything he had said made sense. She would make millions *and* gain the skills to achieve her greatest goal.

So why did she feel there was something she hadn't thought of in this bargain to which she was about to agree? But even if there was, the positives far outweighed any possible negatives. With Des's wedding band on her finger, she would at last control Baron International, something she had wanted for as long as she could remember.

She stopped and looked across the office at Colin. "Okay, it's a deal."

He slowly smiled. "Good decision."

"When do we start?"

"On you, or on our two pieces of land?"

Impatiently she closed the distance between them. "I'll look over your ideas and come up with some of my own. Then we can make another appointment to discuss the land. But for now, I'd like our focus to be on turning me into whatever you think I need to be in order to attract Des."

He came off the desk. "Great. Would tonight be too soon to start?"

She hesitated. Why? she wondered. He was only trying to set into motion what she'd just told him she wanted. "No, tonight would be fine."

"Then I'll be at your house at eight."

"Why?"

"We're going out to dinner, but before we do, I

need to go through your closet and pick out what you should wear.''

"For heaven's sake, why? I go out to dinner at least four times a week.''

"Maybe, but your dinners are always about one of two things—business or one of the charity commit-tees you work on.''

She thought about it and decided that, once again, he was right. "Okay, so how will this be different?''

"Tonight is going to be a *date*." His brown eyes held a golden-colored twinkle that for some reason made her feel warm *and* uneasy inside. "Tell me something, Jill. Can you even remember the last time you went out with a man that had nothing to do with work or charity?''

She tried to recall such an occasion and couldn't. "No, but how hard can a date be?''

"That's what we'll find out tonight. Okay?''

She nodded, once again feeling as though there was something more to this deal than she was seeing. But how could that be? She'd agreed to what Colin wanted, and in turn, he was going to teach her what she needed to know. Quid pro quo. So why was she concerned?

Apparently he read her mind. "Don't worry, Jill. I'll do my best to make sure that, in the end, you get exactly what you want.''

Four

"**I** was right." Colin exited her vast walk-in closet. "You don't have anything appropriate to wear for tonight."

Tapping her foot, Jill stood in the middle of her bedroom, dressed in an ivory silk bathrobe, beneath which she wore neutral-colored bra and panties. Her hair and makeup were already done. She was just waiting for Colin to find something for her to wear of which he approved, and her patience was almost gone. "First of all, what do you mean, you were right?"

"I didn't think I'd find anything for you to wear tonight."

"And how could you possibly know that?" Her irritable tone matched her mood.

"I see you often enough to know what type of clothes you wear. Plus, I was in your closet last night, looking for something warm to put on you, and even though I was in and out pretty fast, I didn't remember seeing anything that would be appropriate for our purposes.''

She inwardly sighed. *Last night.* The more she tried to forget what had happened between the two of them the night before, the more she was reminded. ''Somewhere in that closet there *has* to be something appropriate for our purposes, whatever that means.''

He grinned, and suddenly she remembered how easily that same grin could make a woman melt at his feet.

''Why, Jill, I can't believe you've forgotten. Something that will be appropriate for our purposes means something that will attract Des's attention.''

She blinked. Heaven help her, she *had* forgotten. Ever since this morning, when she had awoken with Colin in bed beside her and discovered he'd held her all night long, she had been focused almost totally on him. That had to stop. ''There must be something in there,'' she said, gesturing toward her closet. ''The contents would stock a clothing store.''

''I agree with that. And by the way, I'm not knocking your taste. It's impeccable.''

She threw out her arms. ''Then what is it?''

''There's no color in your wardrobe. You always wear neutrals. Men like color. Plus, you dress in a very tailored style, which is fine. But every once in a while men enjoy something less tailored, something that shifts and flows and, at the same time, fits closer to your body and perhaps shows a little more than you like to show.''

She crossed her arms and sent him a suspicious look. ''Shows a little more *what?*''

"Flesh, honey. Flesh. I've never seen you look anything less than ladylike, even though I have to admit that sometimes you come up with something that strikes me as discreetly sexy. For our purposes, however, that's not good enough."

Honey? She'd thought she had remembered everything from the night before, but now she recalled that he had called her "honey" several times. She couldn't decide whether she was in the middle of her worst nightmare, or if she was merely taking advantage of a gift from the gods. She was trying to convince herself it was the latter.

After Colin had left her office this afternoon, she had gone over every phrase of their conversation, turning his offer to help her attract Des inside out and upside down, and had still come to the same conclusion. He represented her best chance to get Des. But there was only so much she could let him get away with. "For your information, I've never suffered from a lack of men who've been interested in me."

His brows rose. "Have any of those men been Des?"

Damn. He had her there. She chewed on her bottom lip.

"Exactly my point. We'll go shopping tomorrow, but for tonight, I bought something for you to wear." He disappeared into the hall, then reappeared with a glossy honey-colored dress box tied with a matching satin ribbon. She recognized the name on the box. It was from a very exclusive dress shop that carried only the best. She was relieved. At least the dress wouldn't be a piece of trashy lingerie labeled as outerwear.

He handed her the box. "Go try it on. I'm pretty sure it'll fit. There are shoes in there, too."

She wasn't even going to ask how he had known what dress and shoe size she wore. He was entirely too experienced with women for her peace of mind. She took the box from him and went into her gold-and-cream bathroom. With the door closed behind her, she stared at herself in the mirror, bewildered over her last thought. Why should she care how much experience Colin had with women? She shouldn't. She *didn't*.

With that firmly settled in her mind, she untied the bow, pulled off the lid, parted the honey-hued tissue paper and lifted out a handful of material. It was a deep hot pink and created out of some sort of silky blend. When she put it on over her head, it floated down around her, light as gossamer.

She stood at the full-length mirror, assessing herself, turning this way and that, all the while wondering why she felt so uncomfortable in the dress. There was nothing lewd or vulgar about it, and its designer was world-famous. Deservedly so.

The dress was almost a piece of art, ingeniously constructed so that it took nearly all its shape from her body. Clinging to her in an uninhibited manner, the material crisscrossed her breasts in free-form pleats to a plunging V neckline, then curved inward at her waist. From there, the light-as-air material followed the line of her hips to fall without restraint and end at midcalf. The back had the same plunging V.

The weightless material of the dress, combined with its cut, left her feeling as if she wasn't wearing anything at all.

"How does it look?" Colin called.

"I'm not sure," she muttered. "I'll be out in a minute," she said, more loudly. Or not, she thought.

She couldn't find a single fault with the dress, not the design, the fit or the fabric. But she felt...*exposed.*

She returned to the box and the shoes, which turned out to be the same color as the dress, with three-inch heels that were held to her feet with nothing but straps. Taking a few experimental steps, she found that the shoes felt surprisingly stable *and,* drat it, just her size. As for the size of the dress, it adhered to her body so well it was as if it had been made just for her.

She pulled the honey tissue paper from the box and gave it a good shake, hoping a cover-up of some sort might appear. Unfortunately, only a small pink purse fell out. She scooped it up and gave one last look at her image in the mirror; then, with dread and a strange, expectant flutter in her stomach, she returned to the bedroom.

Colin glanced up, saw her and froze. The expression on his face made her heart stop. *Pure, naked lust.* In all the time she'd known him, she had never seen him look at a woman the way he was looking at her now.

Excitement slammed into her; then her heart thudded. Between her legs, full-blown heat appeared and, embarrassingly, she began to moisten.

It all happened within a matter of seconds; then his naked desire disappeared as if it had never been. But her body still felt its impact, and she was left to try to cope.

"Turn around," he said hoarsely.

Without argument, she did. It was as if he was a puppet master, pulling her strings, and she had no other recourse but to let him control her movements, because she still couldn't manage to get command of her feelings.

"Beautiful." The word came out on a breath.

"Did the…" She chewed on her bottom lip for longer than she would ordinarily have allowed herself. Then she straightened. "Did the dress come with any undergarments?"

"No." Slowly, methodically, his gaze touched her from the top of her head to the tip of her toes. "You need to take off the bra you have on. It shows both in the front and the back."

"I know, and I'm sure I have another bra I can wear with it."

"And now that I think about it, those panties need to go, too. Their line shows through the material."

"I'll find replacements." She tossed the small pink purse onto the bed, managing to land it near the navy one she'd carried to work today, then hurried into her closet.

When Colin walked into the brightly lit closet, she was sorting through a large, shallow drawer filled with bras.

"That dress was never meant for a bra. Besides, you don't need to wear one. You have beautiful breasts."

Her face flushed hot. Her head snapped around. "How do you—" *Last night.* "Never mind. I'll find something. Just get out."

"Okay, but remember—you can't wear anything that will show or ruin the line of the dress."

"How very style-conscious of you."

"That's what I'm here for."

"Get out, Colin."

He tilted his head and looked at her. "Why is your jaw tensed?"

She gave a hollow laugh. "You're kidding, right?" She straightened. "It's this…this dress. It may be designed to attract a man, but I might as well be wearing nothing. And if I *don't* wear a bra or panties, I really *will* be wearing nothing."

"And wearing them would make you feel better?"

"Yes."

Ruefully, he shook his head. "We've got much more work to do than I originally thought."

"If you think for one minute that I'll ever go out of this house without wearing—"

He held up his hand. "Never mind. We'll get to that part later."

"Later?" She almost sputtered.

His gaze lowered and his voice thickened. "As for now, panties with a different line are okay, but don't put on a bra. In fact…" He reached behind her, unsnapped the bra, and before she knew what was happening, he had somehow managed to slide the bra straps down her arms, then with one last tug at the bra's front, it was off and tossed over his shoulder. "There," he murmured, his voice thick and filled with satisfaction. "The bodice looks amazing, clinging to your breasts the way it does."

She fell weakly against the drawer, closing it. "That's quite a party trick. No wonder you're such a hit with women."

He stretched a hand toward her, reaching as close to her as he could without actually touching her, and when he spoke, his hand moved around her breasts, demonstrating his words. "Your breasts are perfect— high…firm…just large enough…"

Heat filled her lungs. She felt as if she was suffocating. "Will you please just get the hell out of here?"

He dropped his hand to his side. "Keep your eye on the prize, honey. This is only the first lesson. I know you're finding it hard, but when you get Des, it'll all be worth it." He paused, his eyes suddenly piercing. "Won't it?"

"*Leave.* And don't call me *honey!*"

He chuckled. "Sure. Anything you say."

As soon as he left, she banged her forehead against a cabinet door several times. If this was only the first lesson, she didn't know if she would survive the rest. This one was definitely baptism by fire.

Yet if she did survive, the rest would be a piece of cake. Plus, Colin had said *when* you get Des. Not *if.* That meant he felt he could teach her how to land Des. If she did, it would all be worth it. Wouldn't it? She frowned to herself. Where had that doubt come from? Of *course* it would all be worth it.

She took a deep breath, slipped on a different pair of panties and positioned herself in front of the closet mirror. Automatically she brushed her hand down the dress, straightening it, then eyed herself critically. Colin had been right again. The dress *did* look better without a bra. Though it wasn't obvious that she wasn't wearing anything beneath it, her breasts filled the bodice perfectly.

She went still. Colin knew the shape and size of her breasts. Last night, the pain and medication had made her responses slow, and she hadn't been able to think straight, yet she hadn't been unconscious. He had undressed her, but he hadn't caressed her. If he had, she would have remembered.

Her breasts began to ache as she thought of his hands closing around her, measuring, weighing. His hands were large, his fingers long. How would they feel around her? She groaned at her wayward thoughts.

"Everything all right?" Colin asked.

"Oh, just peachy keen."

"Peachy, huh?"

She heard the amusement in his voice. Shaking her head at herself, she turned off the closet lights and closed the door behind her.

"You look...remarkable." His arms were crossed over his chest, his expression objective, but she couldn't miss the heat in his eyes.

"Thank you...I think."

He chuckled. "Sorry you're finding this so rough."

She mentally chastised herself. She didn't completely understand why, but she had obviously overreacted to Colin's efforts to help her. "Not rough. Just...different." After the hard, regimented way her father had brought her up, wearing a different type of dress than she was accustomed to and without a bra couldn't even compare.

"Then I hope you won't mind me telling you that the color of your toenails is not right."

"What's wrong with them? They're pink."

"They're too pale."

She jerked up the navy purse and transferred what she would need for the evening to the smaller pink purse. "Be strong, Colin. You'll get over it."

"I'm sure you're right, but there's one more thing I need to do before you're completely ready."

"I can't imagine what it could be. You've seen to every single detail."

He stepped toward her. Instinctively she took a step backward.

He gently smiled. "What are you afraid of, Jill?"

Good question. Was she afraid she was going to enjoy herself? Or learn to like being around him too much? Impossible. "I'm not afraid of anything."

"Good, then stand still for just a minute." He reached out and pulled the hairpins from her head, letting them drop to the cream-colored carpet.

"What on earth are you—"

"Your hair," he muttered. "It's way too severe. *As usual.*" When every last pin was gone, he pushed his fingers through her hair and combed until the dark tresses fell loose and full to her shoulder blades. "Much better. Let's go."

"Oh, uh, wait. I need one more thing." She darted into the closet and reappeared with an ivory, finely crocheted shawl wrapped around her. "The night air might be a little cool." Her expression dared him to tell her differently.

He slowly smiled. "Of course. Let's go."

A sudden thought occurred to her. "Wait. You haven't told me where we're going yet."

"Midnight Blues. It's a brand-new blues club down in Deep Ellum."

"Blues—okay. Then there's one more thing. Please, *please,* tell me we won't run into anyone we know there."

"We won't run into anyone we know there."

Her eyes narrowed suspiciously on him. "Are you sure?"

Amusement glinted in his eyes. "I have to admit, I don't know where all our friends and acquaintances are spending this evening, but the club is new, and most people haven't caught on to it yet.'' The amusement vanished as his gaze darkened and heated. ''Besides, what's the worst thing that can happen? That they see you looking like an incredibly desirable woman?'' He put his hands on her shoulders, and when she started to pull away, his hold tightened. ''Relax, Jill,'' he said, his voice soft. ''You look more beautiful than I've ever seen you look.''

''Don't *touch* that door handle.''

Confused, she glanced around at Colin. ''Why?''

He strolled up with that almost irresistible lazy smile of his, all signs of heat gone from his eyes. ''Because, Jill, a woman always waits for her date to open the car door for her.''

An objection formed in her mouth, but she swallowed it. Politely, she stood aside while he opened the door for her; then she slid in. He tucked the excess of her skirt inside the car, then shut it.

As he circled the car, settled his long frame inside and drove out of her driveway toward downtown, she reflected that she was beginning to understand how the women he dated felt. When he concentrated all his attention on a woman, as he had on her for the past hour or so, he was incredibly sexy.

He glanced at her. ''Allowing me to open the door for you wasn't so hard, was it?''

''Of course not. But since most women are as able as a man to open a door, it's a silly custom.'' She held up her hand in a pacifying gesture. ''But if that little gesture helps to build up a man's ego, then I'll do it—though, as I said before, it's silly.''

He chuckled. ''You sound as if you're suffering.''

''Sorry. It's just that you're asking me to turn one

hundred and eighty degrees on how I think and dress, which must mean that a man, or rather Des, values a woman's looks over a woman's brain. It's rather disheartening.''

"Maybe at first a man is drawn to a woman because of the way she looks. But to keep him beside her without anything else going for her but her looks is a whole different story.''

"Really?'' She'd never thought about it before.

He nodded. "So what I'm trying to do is *soften* you, Jill, and to teach you to accept attention from a man, any man you want—Des, if it turns out he's your heart's desire.''

Des? Heart's desire? What a funny way of putting it, she reflected. Not only funny, but wrong, all wrong. "And you're going to teach me how to attract a man, right? I mean, Des.''

He nodded. "And keep his attention once it's on you. Let's face it, you're a formidable woman who lets all men know, right off the bat, that you're not interested in them—unless, of course, they have something you want for your business.''

"Am I really that bad?''

He smiled gently. "Pretty much.''

She mulled over what he had said. "Did you mean it when you said I looked like a very desirable woman?''

He glanced over at her. "Honey, believe me, that was an understatement.''

A thrill shot through her. She should remind him not to call her honey, but at the moment it was beyond her. She *felt* desirable, she realized with a start, and it had nothing to do with the dress. Surprisingly, it had everything to do with Colin. She wondered if he knew it, then decided he did. It was all part and parcel of the little indoctrination program he was putting her through.

She picked at the hot-pink silk of her skirt in the same way she would pick at lint. "How did you know how this dress would look on me? It probably didn't look like much on a hanger. And not only that, how did you know it would fit me so perfectly? You even found matching shoes that fit."

He shrugged, taking a corner. "Just lucky, I guess."

"Oh, come on. Luck had nothing to do with it. You must have a lot of experience in buying clothes for women."

"Actually, no, but I'm a quick study. And don't forget, I did have the advantage of spending last night with you in bed."

She closed her eyes. She'd walked right into that one. But he needn't worry. If she lived to be a hundred, she doubted she would ever forget, in her fog of pain and medication, that she had slept the night through in his arms. "I'll pay you back for the dress and shoes of course. Every nickel."

"Whatever you like. By the way, did you have a chance to look over my ideas for our two properties?"

There it was. The reminder of the reason he was doing all this, and she supposed she should be relieved. She chewed on her bottom lip. If there was one thing in the world she understood, it was business. So why, then, did she have butterflies in the pit of her stomach and heat crawling through her veins? It was almost as if she was a teenager on her first date.

And why did she have the feeling that learning to

be a femme fatale with Colin as her teacher just might be the hardest thing she had ever tried to do?

From the moment she'd hit puberty, she had known that she was beautiful. She only had to watch the reaction of the boys at her school, and even some men, as she walked into a room or passed by them on the street.

Only her father appeared unmoved by her beauty. In fact, if anything, he seemed to keep her at more of a distance and treat her with slightly more coolness than he did her sisters, although it was so subtle she doubted anyone else saw it. Sometimes she was even able to talk herself into believing it was just her imagination. After all, why would he be harder on her than he was on Kit and Tess? It didn't make sense. But then he would slight her again, and she would know she was right.

Her father never kept any pictures of her mother out, nor did he allow anyone to talk about her in his presence. But once their uncle William had pulled out an old photograph of a breathtakingly lovely young woman and had told her and her sisters that the woman was their mother. Studying the picture, she had realized that she'd been born with her mother's classical beauty. She'd also realized that perhaps the resemblance to her mother might explain her father's attitude toward her. She had always had the impression that her father had never forgiven his wife for having the automobile accident that had killed her.

Nevertheless, since he was the only man whose approval she wanted, she had learned early to disregard her beauty. And like any child seeking love from a parent, she would work all that much harder to please him with her brains and hard work. To her knowledge, she had never succeeded.

He had been dead for many years now. And she had fulfilled the condition of his will, which stated that unless she and her sisters earned *his* idea of a fortune, they would lose their portions of the company. Yet, his powerful, domineering presence remained, and she still lived her life the way he had taught her. It was not only the way she had learned to survive, it was the only way she knew to live.

In order not to be hurt, she had become completely self-contained, emotionally isolating herself from people as much as possible. She didn't even like to be physically touched. No wonder that even the idea of these upcoming lessons in learning to beguile a man was making her nervous.

"Jill?" Colin snapped his fingers in front of her face.

"What?"

"We're here."

"Oh." She glanced around and saw that they were in a parking lot. *"Oh."* She automatically reached for the door handle.

"Uh-uh."

Damn. She waited impatiently for Colin to walk around to her side of the car, open the door and extend his hand toward her. She took it, allowing him to help her out, but not happily. "Tell me something. Does a man's ego really rise or fall on whether or not his date allows him to open the door for her?"

He smiled down at her. "A man's ego is a fragile thing, Jill."

"I don't believe that for a minute. I'd bet money that yours isn't. And I'm sure Des's isn't."

He put his hand on her back and guided her across the parking lot. "Let me put it this way. A man who truly likes and respects a woman enjoys doing things for her, such as opening doors. And usually it makes the woman in question feel honored that the man thinks enough of her to go out of his way to do things for her."

That idea had never even occurred to her, and reflecting on it, she couldn't think of a thing to say.

When they reached the sidewalk, he took her hand. She barely managed to stop herself from pulling away. She couldn't remember ever holding a man's hand before. Odd, she supposed. Most couples held hands, but then, she had never been part of a couple.

Deep Ellum was so named because it consisted of the blocks literally at the end of Elm Street, lying in the shadows of downtown Dallas and stopping at the gates of Fair Park. In its heyday, during the twenties and thirties, Deep Ellum became famous for its many blues clubs. All the greats had come there to play. Since that time, the street and the area had gone through many reincarnations, but always it had remained an alternative to the norm.

Today the term had grown to incorporate 170 acres of previously run-down, deserted warehouses three blocks east of downtown Dallas. But now the warehouses were being turned into high-priced lofts for people who wanted to enjoy a different way of living, and the waiting list was long.

But the main strip remained Elm, and its present-day clubs were the birthplace for many new cutting-edge bands and the home for trendsetting styles. Some of the old shops that had been there for fifty years or more still remained, but other shops now held art galleries, fashion-forward jewelry and clothing boutiques, restaurants, coffee houses and more.

With a firm grasp on her hand, Colin maneuvered them through a mixed crowd, where people seemed to be chatting and laughing with one another, oblivious to the fact that they were blocking pedestrian traffic.

It was hard for her to find one person who didn't have tattoos, or rings in either their noses, eyebrows, tongues or belly buttons, or a combination thereof. Their hairdos ran from bald to spiked, and the hair colors rainbowed from scarlet and orange to blue and gold. But finally she also saw more normal-looking people, even older couples coming out of restaurants or coffee houses.

At one point Colin looked at her and laughed. "Fun, huh?"

"Do you come down here a lot?"

"Maybe not a lot, but whenever there's something interesting going on, and there usually is, I try to come down. Don't you own quite a few of the old warehouses down here that are being converted?"

She nodded. "I bought up as many as were available, but I've never come down here at night."

"Maybe after this you'll want to."

He angled them toward a black doorway. As soon as he opened the door, music sailed out. She hesitated only because the interior of the club was so dark, but Colin kept her hand in his and ushered her into the club.

Inside, Colin stopped to talk with a big, burly man who had walked over to meet them as if he was an old friend of Colin's. While the two men talked, her eyes gradually began to adjust so that she could see the stage.

A young, white, skinny guy played the guitar. An older black man sat on a straight-back chair slightly to the right and behind him, playing another. There were also a drummer, a saxophonist and a pianist, but they might as well not have been there, as far as the two guitarists were concerned. They were each taking different parts of the song, trading licks as if they could read each other's minds, making their guitars talk to each other in a language that everyone there seemed to understand at some level. She was no expert, but even *she* knew she was hearing something transcendent.

She felt the shawl being whisked off her shoulders; then Colin led her toward the back of the room. She glanced at him just long enough to see that he had her shawl over his arm, then returned to inspecting the club.

Blue neon made random pathways of light across the ceiling and walls. The neon revealed large, stark, black-and-white photos of blues legends, all holding their beloved guitars. She recognized the names— Robert Johnson, Muddy Waters, Howlin' Wolf and other masters. Other pictures showed Billie Holiday and Bessie Smith.

Interspersed among the portraits were other black-and-white pictures of old black men, sitting in rocking chairs on their run-down front porches, playing their guitars. The pictures plainly said that the men might not have glass for their windows, but their souls were full, fed by their guitars and the music they made. Other pictures showed black people walking up and down rows of cotton, stooped over, picking and filling their burlap bags. Under all these pictures were brass plaques that simply said The Birth of the Blues.

Colin's hand extended past her and pointed to an empty booth of midnight-blue leather. She slid in, and Colin slipped in beside her. Her nerves jumped at his closeness.

The music was loud, but a long way from earsplitting. Nevertheless, he put his mouth close to her ear. "Move over a few more inches and give me some room."

She gestured to the other side of the booth. "What about sitting over there?"

He shook his head and gave the waitress a smile as she walked up to them. Jill had no choice but to move closer to the wall, though it did no good, because he simply followed her until his side was against hers.

The blond waitress, who had an ample bosom and a pin on her white blouse that spelled out Maggie, gave Colin her entire attention. But Jill did manage to get in her order of white wine. Colin ordered beer.

As Maggie sashayed off, leaving menus, Colin slid his arm behind her along the top of the booth's leather back. "What do you think of the place?" he asked, leaning toward her, his mouth once again close to her ear, his breath warm on her skin.

She swallowed a feeling of panic. He had her pinned against the wall and the back of the booth. He was too close, too male, too overwhelming, and though he was no longer actually touching her, he was. In every way she could think of. Somehow she managed a smile. "Great music."

His smile held such genuine pleasure it almost took her breath away. "I'm so glad you like it. I love it."

"Those two—" she nodded toward the two guitarists "—are something special."

"What?"

Even though she didn't understand why he couldn't hear her, she positioned her lips close to his ear. "The two guitarists are really special."

He turned his head to reply so fast that he caught her off guard, and his lips brushed hers before she had a chance to turn her head. She literally jumped about half an inch. He placed his left hand on her forearm and slowly rubbed his palm back and forth over it. "You've got to learn not to flinch every time a man touches you."

She looked down at his hand on her arm and nodded. He was right. It would never do to jerk away from Des. But then, this was Colin. "Normally I do much better."

He nodded in agreement. "You do—as long as you don't perceive the person to be a threat to you in some way."

It was an odd thing for him to say, and probably true, though she had never bothered to analyze why she did things. But Colin was fast changing that and, in the process, making her feel extremely vulnerable.

She did her best to edge away from him, failed, and decided to look around at the other patrons. As soon as he had told her they were going to a club in Deep Ellum, she had been certain she would feel out of place in the dress he had bought her. But, to her surprise, she didn't.

The people there spanned all ages and wore all manner of dress. There were those who wore clothing even dressier than she and Colin wore, as if they might have just come from the Morton H. Myerson

Hall, where they had attended a symphony, or perhaps the Music Hall, where they might have attended an opera or a musical.

She thought she even caught a glimpse of a few of the Dallas Cowboys, including the quarterback, at a back table. Normally she would expect them to be mobbed, but here, everyone was leaving everyone else alone. They were there for the music and the company. And Colin had even been right about something else. She didn't think she knew a single person there. Her spirits lightened.

Maybe she could relax, after all, and enjoy herself.

"You need to be looking at me."

She started. "Excuse me?"

"It's a basic rule, Jill. Your attention should be on the man you are with."

"Oh. Well, it's just that the club is so interesting."

"And during conversations, you should hang on his every word, as if he's the most fascinating person you've ever met."

She slowly exhaled. Just as she had decided she might be able to relax and actually enjoy herself, Colin had to remind her that they were there as part of her lessons. She was beginning to hate the word *lesson*. "Look, you can *tell* me things like that—after all, that's the bargain we struck. But do I actually have to *do* the things you say?"

His half smile gave her a peek at his dimple. "You absolutely do. Otherwise, how are you going to learn? I mean, if you don't practice these things with me, you might do them wrong when you're with Des."

He was right, she supposed. Damn it.

Five

The band was on a break, and Billie Holiday's voice filled the club with her heartbreak as she sang "I Don't Stand a Ghost of a Chance with You," a song about her unrequited love for a man.

She didn't understand that kind of love, Jill reflected. How could a woman continue to love a man if he didn't love her? It didn't make sense, and it certainly wouldn't be productive.

She and Colin had finished dinner, though she hadn't eaten much. The fare was basically Cajun, and the few bites she'd taken from her plate had been very good. But she was having problems relaxing. Everything about Colin was overwhelmingly compelling. He was the most intensely virile man she had ever known.

Why hadn't she seen it before now? With her next

breath, she answered her own question. Because she hadn't *allowed* herself to. And now she knew why.

Instinct had led her to keep Colin at arm's length, and in retrospect, it had been a wise decision. She completely understood now why her female acquaintances tried so hard to get, then keep, his attention on them, and why they would become so distraught when inevitably, politely, he slipped away from them.

She was after another man, but that still didn't make her immune to Colin. Not by a long shot. Why? she wondered. She'd had men come after her before—powerful, attractive, important men—yet she'd had no trouble handling them. If it would gain her something, she would play them along until they had served their purpose, then she would walk away.

So why couldn't she be that objective with Colin?

Intellectually, she knew she had his full attention because of a business deal they had made, but emotionally, she could feel herself coming dangerously close to being completely caught up in him. How could that be?

She touched her forehead. She needed to regain control of herself and remember why she was with him in the first place.

She felt his hand touch her shoulder. "Are you getting a headache?"

He looked so concerned that, before she knew it, she had rushed to reassure him. "No, not at all."

"Are you sure? The music isn't too loud for you?"

"No, really, I'm fine."

Now another Billie Holiday song, one that made even less sense to her, was coming over the speakers. "Don't Explain" was about a woman who loved her man so completely that she didn't care what he did, including cheating on her. In her joy and in her pain, the woman would still continue to be his.

She had a vague idea about what love between a man and a woman would require. She wasn't kidding herself. She didn't think she and Des would ever have the kind of marriage her sister Tess and her husband, Nick, had. For one thing, she didn't even begin to understand that kind of marriage. The two of them together seemed so complete, such a whole. Every time she saw her sister, Tess practically glowed with happiness. But as for herself, she wasn't certain it would be worth it to give up so much of herself to another person.

However, as soon as Des agreed to marry her, she would be willing to do her part. If they each went into the marriage with open eyes and minds, they would get along just fine. But she didn't think she could ever love a man to such an extent that nothing else would matter.

"What are you thinking about?"

She was becoming accustomed to Colin's soft, husky voice, so instead of starting, as she might have at the beginning of the evening, she merely turned her head and looked at him. "The lyrics of the song."

"Powerful, aren't they?"

"Yes, and delivered with a wealth of emotion few of today's artists can match."

"Ah, but you have to know the blues to sing them. Plus, there was and will always be only one Lady Day. Unfortunately, she knew all about the blues."

She stared at him, thinking about what he'd said. Her upbringing had been rough, but she'd survived, just as her sisters had, though each in her own way. She probably wasn't as well adjusted as some people were, but she had never allowed herself the luxury of self-pity and had always succeeded in what she set out to do. So she had no self-reference for the blues, but of one thing she was absolutely certain: she would never love a man in the way Billie Holiday sang about.

She believed in learning what you could from the past, then pushing forward to accomplish your goals for the future. Which was why she was here tonight, she reminded herself. She took a sip of her wine.

She felt a finger beneath her chin turning her head to face him. "What kind of blues are those lyrics conjuring up for you?"

"None," she answered quickly, perhaps too quickly.

"No?"

"No." She shook her head in emphasis, freeing herself from his touch.

"Have you ever loved someone that much?"

How in the world did he read her mind like he did? It was not only disconcerting, it was annoying. "Have you?" she asked, deciding to throw the potentially explosive question back at him.

He slowly smiled, his eyes fixed so firmly on her that she had to consciously stop herself from squirming. "Maybe."

It was the last thing in the world she had expected him to say. But now that she thought about it, his answer might explain a question none of her women acquaintances had been able to answer. If he had been deeply in love with a woman before he had come into their group, and something had happened to ruin that love, it would explain why he walked away from a woman every time he sensed she was getting serious.

Maybe his heartbreak still hurt too much. Funny, she reflected, but he was the last man on earth she would imagine allowing a woman to break his heart.

"Who?" she asked, curious, but also on some vague level disturbed.

"Why do you want to know?"

"Because you're a hard man to figure out."

"And do you want to figure me out?"

She shrugged, uncertain what to say. "Some of the women you've dated would like to."

"That wasn't what I asked."

The truth was, now that she'd spent some time with him, she *would* like to know what made him tick. And the thing she would like to know most was what kind of woman would it take to win his heart?

Amusement glittered in Colin's eyes as he reached out and stroked his fingers through her hair. "*You* haven't answered *my* question. Is that because you don't know or don't want to say?"

"I'm not sure." It was the most honest answer she could give him, and he seemed to understand.

His smile broadened. "Let's dance."

"Dance?" She glanced toward the dance floor and saw that it was full of couples completely absorbed in each other, swaying and moving to the music. She took a sip of her wine. "Why?" Her mind was still on the mystery woman in Colin's past.

"Because it would be fun, or isn't that a good enough reason?"

"This is business. We're not on a date, Colin." A sudden realization hit her. She just assumed the woman was in his past, but what if she was still around? She frowned, troubled in a way she couldn't understand.

"No, we're not, but you need to learn how to dance the way Des would expect you to."

That got her attention. "What do you mean?"

He took her hand. "Come on. I'll show you."

Before she could protest, he had her hand and was drawing her across the seat of the booth to her feet. Maybe she *should* have claimed a headache, she realized belatedly.

"I don't need lessons in dancing, Colin. I know how."

He swung her into his arms. "I suppose you do, after a fashion. But you only dance with a man as long as he doesn't hold you close."

"So?" Without the stage lights, the club was darker, more intimate, making it seem as if each couple on the dance floor had their own world where no one else could enter.

"So what's the point of dancing at arm's length?"

"For one thing, it's more civilized. For instance, if you can look at your partner, you can actually carry on a conversation with him."

With that enigmatic half smile of his, he slowly shook his head. "You know what I think?"

"No." But at that moment, she would have given a lot to know.

"I think it's a very good thing for you that I came along."

She couldn't help it—she laughed. "There's certainly nothing wrong with your ego, is there?"

"No, but there's something wrong with the way you're dancing." He pulled her tightly against him. "*This* is the way you dance with a man." He pressed his mouth to her ear. "And if you want to have a conversation with him, *this* is the way to do it."

Each word he spoke feathered warm air against her hair and into the sensitive shell of her ear. Tingles raced down her spine. Instinctively she tried to pull away, but he was quicker; anticipating what she would do, he simply tightened his hold on her. "Trust me, Jill. Des will expect you to be this close to him, or closer, especially if you expect him to marry you."

She was certain he was right, and to his credit, it wasn't something she would have thought about if he hadn't brought it to her attention, but at the moment, Des was the farthest thing from her mind. Colin, with his musky, woodsy, all-male smell, was guiding her to a place, both mentally and physically, where she was quite sure she shouldn't go. But she seemed to have no choice.

A slow song by an artist she didn't recognize played over the sound system, saturating the club with music and lyrics that wailed about painful wants and deep, complex love.

Colin pulled her arms around his neck, then slipped one of his hands beneath the V at the back of the waistline of her dress to settle on her bare skin; with the palm of his other hand against her buttocks, he pulled her pelvis into his. Feelings so hot they stole her breath from her lungs washed through her. She closed her eyes as she attempted to withstand the on-slaught of pure longing that was flowing through her like molten lava.

"Relax," he breathed into her ear. "You're safe. You're with me, and we're in the middle of a public place, surrounded by people."

He didn't understand, she thought helplessly. For that matter, neither did she. But for the first time in her life, she was afraid of her own feelings.

And the music…it was low and sexy, with a beat that throbbed and slipped into your bloodstream until you were part of the song and it was part of you. The singer's voice was raw and ravaged, but still, he held nothing back. With the music and the lyrics, he was opening himself up in such a way that the listener could almost hear his heart bleed.

She'd never experienced anything remotely like it. The song, Colin—both were conjuring up feelings from deep within her she'd never known she had. She tried her best to summon up her normal, protective coating of reserve, but it was no use. The music decreed that their movements be as slow and hotly sensual as the song, and Colin was obeying, dancing them both deeper and deeper into the song and each other.

He held her firmly against his strong body, her breasts pressed against his chest with only thin fabric separating skin from skin. His hand caressed her bare back. Lower, she could feel his hard arousal. Her blood thickened; her legs weakened. She might have fallen if he hadn't been holding her to him as if they were one.

And for this space of time, they were. Her body and everything that made up who she was had melted into him, and there wasn't a thing she could do about it. She didn't even have to think in order to follow his dance steps. It was automatic. As they swayed together, her pelvis moved in the exact direction his did, swinging right, left, then erotically circling.

Heat swirled in and around her, and she tightened her arms around his neck and threaded her fingers up into his hair. Want was building in her, and she didn't have a clue how to stop it, assuage it. His arousal was growing, but he made no effort to pull away. As for her, she was incapable. She didn't even want to. His size and shape were now indelibly imprinted onto her skin and into her brain. She had seen him in his tight-fitting briefs. Now she didn't even have to imagine what was beneath them. Some part of her brain was telling her that this couldn't continue, while another screamed that it had to.

Then he thrust his leg between hers and pulled her onto his muscular thigh. Pleasure, unimaginable pleasure, shocked through her, but he gave her no chance to recuperate. Taking her with him, he began to snake sinuously downward, then undulate back up. Blindly she emulated his every twist, breathless at the constant feel of her panties rubbing against his thigh.

Again and again, they did the same thing, and all the while, the heat and pleasure that had taken her over climbed ever higher. On a dance floor, surrounded by couples, they were making love. Heavy, throbbing heat ached between her legs. Need and desire held her in a grip so strong she might never escape. She didn't think she could take any more. Something had to happen. Something, someone, had to help her. And not surprisingly, Colin seemed to know exactly what she was feeling.

At the same time that she went limp against him, he stopped and straightened. And as the music and dancers continued around them, he simply held her trembling body against his own. With one hand holding her upright at her waist, he used the other to rub up and down her back, soothing her.

Minutes later, hours later, he pulled slightly away from her, though his arm still firmly held her at the waist. He raised a hand to her jaw and tilted her face up to his. "Maybe that's enough for now."

She couldn't speak. She couldn't even look at him. Somehow she found the strength to wrench herself from his arms and make her way back to their booth. There she dropped onto the cushioned midnight-blue leather and reached for her wine. Her hands were trembling so badly that some of it sloshed out of the glass. Nevertheless, she drank the rest of it straight down.

"Coffee might help more."

She looked across the table and realized Colin had taken a seat there. Thank heavens he hadn't resumed his previous seat beside her. She wouldn't have been able to stand his closeness. Even now, with the table separating them, she thought she could still feel his heat. Or maybe it was her own.

His hands were folded together on the table. He looked perfectly composed, but his chest was rising and falling faster than usual. He hadn't been unaffected. The fact gave her a portion of satisfaction, but not much.

"I'd rather just leave."

He stared at her for a long moment, and she prayed that, just this once, he wouldn't be able to see what was going on inside her. Because if he could, he would see that a heated desire was rampaging through her body, and that out on the dance floor, she had come to realize that he and only he could assuage her desire. But finally he nodded, and she let out a long shaky breath of relief.

"Fine. Just let me pay our bill."

Within minutes she had her shawl around her and he was ushering her out of the club. Outside, she stopped, needing to orient herself. The streetlights seemed extraordinarily bright after the blue neon lights of the club. And the scene on the sidewalks was, if anything, more crowded than it had been when they had entered hours before.

Hours? Had it only been hours? She took a deep breath of the fresh air. It seemed as if she had lived a lifetime in the club. She felt Colin's hand at her back and stepped away from it.

"The car's not far away," he murmured, gesturing in the direction of the parking lot.

She was drained, with no energy left, yet she managed to put one foot in front of the other, and soon Colin was opening the car door for her. She slid into the seat, then watched numbly as he bent to move the overflow of her skirt into the car so that it wouldn't get caught when he shut the door.

Neither of them spoke on the drive home. Jill used the time to regain her strength, her sanity and her composure, a feat not easily accomplished. But by the time they reached her home, she had been able to come to at least one conclusion.

He pulled the car into her circular drive, braked and turned off the ignition. Silence and the beat of her heart were all Jill could hear. She looked down at her interlocked hands, knowing what she had to say, but waiting, though she wasn't quite sure for what. Colin unbuckled his seat belt, then angled his body toward her. Without even turning her head, she could feel his assessing gaze on her, waiting....

She didn't have the nerves left for a waiting game, so she said what she had to. "I think I've had enough lessons."

"I disagree. We have at least another two or three full days' worth. Possibly four."

Her head jerked around. *"Days?"*

He nodded. "Originally I had planned to stretch the lessons out over a couple of weeks, but after tonight, I've decided that we should accelerate our schedule."

After tonight. That said it all. Out on the dance floor, in his arms, she'd come undone. He'd entered into what he thought was a business agreement, and the first time he had taken her into his arms, she had melted into him. Quite obviously, he wanted their lessons to be over.

"You're going to have to clear your appointments for the next few days."

"Clear my…" The words clogged her throat. "Look, I have no idea what you have in mind, but I think tonight was enough."

"What's bothering you, Jill?" He leaned closer to her. "What's really, down deep, bothering you? That you don't understand what happened between us tonight?"

Once again he had read her mind, so why bother denying what he already knew? "That's one thing," she said slowly.

"Which is exactly *why* you need more lessons. You're not accustomed to a man's touch, *or* dancing closely, *or* anything remotely sexual. And if you know Des at all, you know that he is going to want his wife to respond to him, both in and out of bed. Just in case you didn't know it, that's what happens when two people fall in love."

She cleared her throat. "I know, but I also know Des may not ever love me."

"And you're willing to settle for that? A loveless marriage?"

"Of course." Her answer was automatic, one she'd had in her mind for a long time. "But I would be willing to, uh, respond to him. I mean, I know sex is part of any marriage, but I also know...or rather, *think,* that maybe in our case, we could also have a marriage that is more about business than—"

His roar of laughter interrupted her. "If that's what you truly think, then, honey, you need my lessons more than even I thought. How could you know so little about the man you think you want to spend the rest of your life with? Des is not only going to want love and sex and babies, he's going to want much more than that."

Her brows drew together. What was left? "Like what?"

"Like a companion and a friend, for one."

"That's two." *Babies.* She hadn't even considered that. And *love.* Would Des really want love? She had thought he would understand a marriage arranged for the convenience of a business; plus, he had to know how happy it would make Uncle William if he married one of his nieces. But now Colin was saying that wasn't enough.

Suddenly she felt the beginnings of a migraine. She had to get into the house without Colin realizing that she had a headache coming on. The last thing she needed was a repeat of last night.

As for tonight... She couldn't allow her mind to follow that thought. Abruptly she opened the car door, slid out and slammed it shut.

"Wait." Colin quickly got out of the car and was

by her side just as she was inserting her key into her front-door lock.

"I'll think over what you've said and call you in the morning." She turned the key and pushed the door open.

With his hand, he turned her face up to his. Alarmingly, her first instinct was to lean into his hand for the comfort of his warm caress. *Lord, when had she become such a slow learner?* She jerked away, stepped into her house and started to close the door. Colin's well-placed foot stopped her.

"I know tonight upset you, Jill, and I also know why. But all it proves is that you really haven't thought through this plan of yours. You don't have the slightest idea how to go about getting and keeping Des."

"I'll do whatever I have to." Again an automatic response, but this time it tripped her up.

"Good. Then I'll pick you up here at nine in the morning. Be ready."

Panic hit. "Wait. I haven't even decided whether I'm going to continue with these lessons."

He stepped over the threshold and ran his thumb over her bottom lip. "But you will. You will." Then suddenly he slipped his hands along her cheeks and lowered his mouth to hers. His tongue thrust into her mouth, and heat exploded inside her. Once again, he had easily taken possession of her feelings. She wanted to cry at her lack of control, but she also wanted to learn more about what it felt like to kiss him.

His lips were full and firm, his taste heady, like the finest wine, and the inside of his mouth was moist and warm. He kissed with a surety that spoke of experience as his tongue delved deeper and deeper, engaging hers in an intimate, sexual dance of heat and desire. She closed her hands over his wrists to steady herself.

When he finally raised his head, he whispered, "Another lesson. At the very *least,* Des will expect a kiss at the end of your first date. After that..." His shrug explained perfectly.

The headache was becoming stronger, and she wasn't going to make last night's mistake in thinking she could fight it with only her will. She had to get upstairs as soon as possible and take something for it. She had never known why they came, but the aftermath of tonight had certainly left her stressed. "I'll call you in the morning," she repeated.

"I'll *see* you then," he murmured, and with another soft kiss he was gone.

She closed the door and leaned back against it for support. No man had ever kissed her the way Colin just had. No man had ever held her, touched her, treated her, the way he had tonight. And because of it, she somehow knew she would never be the same.

Six

Jill awoke tired, but with no headache hangover. Taking the medicine at the first sign of the migraine last night, then going to bed, had been the best thing she could have done for herself. She just hated being so dependent on medicine, or admitting that there was an aspect of her life over which she had no control. But by catching the headache early, she had ensured she hadn't had to take any of the heavy-duty medicine she'd had to resort to the night before, when Colin had spent the night with her.

With a groan, she reached for a spare pillow and pressed it over her face. Even as she did it, she knew she wasn't accomplishing anything. Besides, it wasn't like her to try to hide from anything or anyone. Not for a very long time.

But Colin…

With another groan, she threw the pillow across the

room. It was time to start her day. She sat up and pushed the hair from her eyes. Why was she so tired? Then she remembered and collapsed back on the bed. Erotic, disturbing dreams of Colin had filled her night.

That settled the matter. She needed to get out of their business agreement. She hated like blazes to admit it, even to herself, but she couldn't handle another evening like the one they had shared at Midnight Blues.

She reached for another pillow but couldn't find one, so she settled for covering her face with her hands. What was wrong with her? She couldn't hide. She had learned that lesson well when she had been small.

Back then she would crawl into her closet and shut the door, thinking that if her father couldn't find her, she could escape the ordeal of their nightly dinners. It was her secret. As far as she knew, even Tess and Kit didn't know.

The only person who did was the woman who was their housekeeper at the time. She had always known where to find her. The woman wasn't unkind, but even she had been intimidated by her father, so she would straighten Jill's clothes and shoo her downstairs.

There, sitting as straight as they could make their little bodies, she and her sisters would be grilled about their day by their father. In turn, they each would have to tell him what they had learned that day in school and recount their participation in any scholastic or physical competitions. If they couldn't report a win, or the top grade in their class, they would feel the iciness of his disapproval, which was formidable. Invariably she left the table with her stomach in knots.

Later she would lie in bed, hungry, trying to think of ways she could do better the next day.

As soon as she and her sisters were old enough, he saw that they were involved in individual sports, such as tennis or golf, and he would stage competitions among the three of them, pitting them against one another. To this day, she refused to play any kind of sport. She had buried her competitive nature in her business pursuits.

In fact, until Tess married a year and a half ago, Tess, Kit and she would fight tooth and nail to be the one who, at the end of Baron International's fiscal year, had made the most money for the company. But since Tess's marriage, Tess was so blissed out she no longer even tried. Her withdrawal made the competition a lot less fun. As for Kit, who knew what was up with her these days?

No. Hiding never worked. Besides, she wasn't afraid of Colin. She would simply tell him there would be no more lessons, and he would have no choice but to accept her decision.

With a sigh, Jill forced herself to get up. It was past time to start her day.

She had taken exactly three steps when she hesitated and something made her look back at the bed. Her mouth fell open. She'd never seen her sheets in such a tangle. In fact, the whole bed was a mess. The contents of her erotic dreams came rushing back to her, and her face warmed. Hurriedly she made the bed.

"May I see my appointment list, please?"

"You bet." With brisk efficiency, her assistant laid

a brown leather folder in front of her. "This is your day."

Jill opened the folder. Her first appointment wasn't for another hour, but once they started, they were scheduled back to back. At least she had an hour to return calls, review reports and check on several projects she had under way. "Thanks, Molly.

"Do you have something else for me? Because if not, I'm still working on the Barstow report."

"That's fine." As Molly left the office, Jill lifted a cup and sipped at the decaffeinated coffee Molly always freshly brewed for her. There were mornings when she would have killed for a good strong cup of regular coffee, but because of her headaches, the doctor had banned them.

"Good morning."

She almost choked on the coffee. *"Colin."*

He bypassed the chairs and settled himself on a corner of the desk. "Great morning, isn't it?"

Molly immediately reappeared in the doorway. "Mr. Wynne? Did you have an appointment?"

It was Molly's polite way of letting the intruder know he wasn't scheduled. Jill was much less polite. "What in the hell are you doing here?"

Colin flashed Molly a grin. "Does she swear like that very often? Never mind. Before you offer, I'd love a cup of coffee, thank you. Oh, and make mine black and fully leaded."

Molly looked at Jill. With a sigh, she nodded. Molly disappeared, but left the door open.

Colin's sudden appearance had instantly caused her composure to disintegrate, but Jill managed to quickly pull herself together. She sat back in her chair, folded her arms beneath her breasts and gave him a hard look. "Would you like me to repeat the question?"

"Thanks, but no thanks. I heard the first time."

"And the answer is?"

"Fact of the matter is, we *did* have an appointment this morning. Remember? I said I'd see you at nine." He glanced at the gold watch on his wrist. "It is now fifteen minutes after nine. Sorry I'm a little late, but I dropped by your house first. I was sure I had said I would pick you up there. My fault, I'm sure. I must have said here." The gold streaks in his brown eyes suddenly became more pronounced, more mesmerizing. "But then, I was a little preoccupied with the evening we had just spent together."

She sat very still, willing herself not to blush. "You shouldn't be here, Colin. I distinctly remember saying that I'd *call* you this morning."

He gave a nonchalant nod toward the sun currently flooding in through her office's floor-to-ceiling windows, which offered a spectacular view of downtown Dallas. "Well, I don't know about you, but *that* is what I call morning."

Molly returned, carrying his coffee. He took it from her with a smile. "Thanks. Listen, Molly, please correct me if I'm wrong, but it's morning, right?"

"Right." Puzzled, she glanced at Jill, her brows raised in question. When Jill didn't respond, she asked, "Anything else?"

Jill shook her head in resignation. "No, that's it for now."

Molly left and this time closed the door behind her.

"I had planned to call you, Colin, but it's been a busy morning." A well-placed little white lie from time to time never hurt anything, and in this case it would help.

"And I said I would *see* you, but no matter. I'm flexible." He reached into his jacket pocket, pulled out a thin cell phone and held it out to her. "Want to call me?"

"You know, I never realized before just how impossible you are." She pushed away from the desk and stood. He was looking only moderately spectacular this morning, she reflected with annoyance, along with appearing completely rested.

The lightweight sport jacket he wore perfectly complemented his chocolate-brown slacks and tan shirt, unbuttoned at his throat. And as usual, the sun had managed to turn his golden-brown hair to a dark honey. As for his eyes, since she had spotted the intensity of their gold streaks a minute ago, she was trying very hard not to look into them. She was too afraid she would see something that would remind her of last night.

Last night. That made two nights in a row she needed to forget.

She turned her head away from him. The Dallas skyline had always been a soothing sight to her, but for some reason it just wasn't working at the moment. Maybe because she could only see Colin in her mind's eye. "I did what I said I'd do. I thought over the idea of continuing the lessons, and I've decided to stop."

"No guts, huh?"

An irritating response delivered in a soft, almost tender manner. How was she supposed to react to that combination?

Barely contained anger seemed to be the winner.

She looked at him over her shoulder. "It's got nothing to do with guts. I made my decision based on business considerations. First of all, there's no way I can clear my appointments for the next few days."

"What's the matter? Afraid Dallas will fall down without your constant vigilance?"

"And secondly," she said, returning her gaze to the skyline, "I've decided I don't need any more lessons. I told you I'm a quick study, and I am. You've given me more than enough to go on."

"Honey, you're still at the starting gate."

She whirled around. "*Don't* call me honey. And what do you mean, the starting gate? After last night—" She stopped herself. Any mention of anything that concerned what had happened at the club could prove dangerous.

"After last night, what?"

Damn. She'd made the mistake of looking into his eyes, and she'd seen heat flare in them at the mention of last night. She managed to shrug. "It was fun and quite informative, but I can take it from here." Surely there were books she could read on the subject. She would have Molly search the Internet bookstores. "Naturally I won't renege on our business agreement. We'll develop our land jointly." She would assign one of her top people to it, but there was no way she was going to personally work with Colin.

"How extremely ethical of you, but I'm not letting you out of the other half of our deal. I feel a moral obligation to continue, plus—"

"Moral obligation? Give me a break. And while you're at it, consider yourself released."

"*Plus* last night you told me you'd do anything to get Des. I've never known you to exaggerate. There-

fore, I'm taking you at your word. Now—'' he shot
back his cuff and glanced at his watch ''—it's nearly
nine-thirty. We're already running late.'' He slipped
off the desk. ''Let's go.''

She must have missed something. ''Go? Go
where?''

''I've made some appointments for you. Have you
cleared your calendar for the next few days as I told
you to?''

''No, of course not.''

Before she knew it, he was around the desk, her
hand was in his, and he was leading her out of her
office. He opened her office door and breezed through
Molly's smaller office to the door that led to the re-
ception area. ''Hi, Molly. Please cancel Ms. Baron's
appointments for the next few days. Great coffee, by
the way. Thanks a lot.'' He opened her office door.
''Bye, Molly.''

Molly stared after him with a stupefied expression
on her face. ''Jill?''

''I, uh…''

He briefly paused and gazed down at her. ''Just do
it, Jill. Please. I promise you, what's going to happen
today is not going to be near as hard on you as last
night. In fact, if you allow yourself to, you'll enjoy
it.''

''Say the word, Jill, and I'll call the police.''

Great, just great. Molly was in full-fledged protective mode. It was the last thing she wanted. She could
take care of herself. She would either cope with whatever Colin had planned for today, or she would walk
away and call for a cab back to the office. ''It's okay,
Molly. I'm fine.''

She saw Colin flash her assistant a smile that had

brought more than one woman to her knees, but he hadn't come up against Molly's maternal leanings. And apparently he realized the same thing.

"I promise you she's in no danger, nor will she be," he said to Molly. "Have a great day."

"Wait. My purse—it's back in my office."

"That's okay. You're not going to need it."

Now she was curious and, heaven help her, more than a little intrigued. After this was all over, she should probably seriously consider some sort of mental-health care.

"Are you comfortable, Ms. Baron?"

The low, soothing voice of Helen, her assigned masseuse, irritated her. "As comfortable as I can be, half-naked, lying facedown on a massage table with a stranger's hands on me."

"I gather you've never had a massage before."

"That's correct." She'd never had time, nor did she now. What was more, she couldn't believe she had allowed Colin to drag her to this day-of-beauty salon.

"I'm not hurting you, am I?"

"No." In truth, the experience so far wasn't altogether unpleasant. The room was dimly lit. Soft, lilting music played somewhere. But she didn't have time for this indulgence. Plus, she couldn't figure out what having a massage had to do with getting Des.

"You're very, very tense. I can feel it in your muscles. So just try to relax and let me do my job."

She lifted her head off the table and looked hopefully back over her shoulder. "You wouldn't happen to have a cell phone in here, would you?"

"No, Ms. Baron." Helen gently pushed her back

down. "Conducting business at the same time I'm giving you a massage would be counterproductive. Besides, even the busiest of people find that an occasional day here at Jacqui's is beneficial. But you have to give yourself a chance. So, please, just try to relax and let me see if I can get these knots out of your shoulders."

She yawned as Helen rubbed more warm oil into her back. Despite her protestations to the contrary last night, Colin probably felt he couldn't count on her to fulfill her side of their business agreement unless he fulfilled his. Fortunately, that was an easy fix. As soon as she returned to the office, she would put her lawyers to work on drawing up the agreement. Then Colin would *have* to believe her.

Where was he, anyway? The last time she'd seen him, he had been in the main salon, waving her goodbye, as the very beautiful Jacqui, the spa owner, had escorted her into the massage room with a graciousness that was an art unto itself. She sighed. If she only had her cell phone, she could...

"Ms. Baron? Ms. Baron?"
"Yes?" She forced open her eyes. "What is it?"
"The massage is over."
"It is?" Disappointment tinged her voice.
As the massage had continued, she remembered going into a kind of twilight rest, where she felt as if she were drifting on a cloud. Every once in a while she would become aware of Helen's heavenly touch as the woman worked her fingers up and down her body, murmuring occasionally about knots. And she'd been conscious enough to turn over when Helen had

asked her. But after that, she'd sunk back into her cloud. And now she couldn't feel a bone in her body.

"Sit up slowly," Helen cautioned. "You may feel somewhat dizzy at first, but it will pass in a moment."

She sat up just fine, but immediately wanted to lie down again for another hour of massage. She couldn't remember the last time she had felt this relaxed. But Helen was carefully urging her off the table, even going so far as to kneel down and guide her feet into a pair of peach terry-cloth slippers—peach and green being the spa's colors. The slippers matched the robe she put on a moment later.

Helen straightened and beamed at her. "Do you feel better?"

"Yes, thank you very much. You're truly gifted."

With a pleased nod, Helen led her out of the room. "Follow me. Your facial is next."

"Do you know where Mr. Wynne is?" He had assured her that he would not leave the premises. At the time, her theory had been that he had brought her there and he could damn well stay as long as she did. He'd laughed and agreed.

"No, I'm sorry, I don't."

"Here we are." Helen pushed open another door in a hall that seemed lined with endless doors, and Jill entered another dimly lit room to see three green-smocked women waiting for her. There was also the most comfortable-looking lounge chair she had ever seen. "Ladies, she's all yours."

Helen left, quietly closing the door behind her.

A woman with beautiful silver hair came forward. "My name's Mary, Ms. Baron. I'll be doing your facial." She turned and introduced the other two ladies, Cordelia and Alyssa.

"Hello," she said politely, and received a duet of hellos in return.

"While I'm doing your facial," Mary said, "Cordelia will be giving you a manicure and Alyssa will be doing your pedicure."

"How efficient," Jill said with true approval.

"Some of our clients like to linger all day, while others would rather not," Mary explained. "Mr. Wynne said you fell into the latter category."

"He did, did he?" Colin knew her entirely too well. "Do you happen to know where he is?"

"I believe he's in one of our private salons with Jacqui."

Private salon? "Do you know what they're doing?"

"No, I'm afraid I don't."

Why should she care what Colin was doing? With the beautiful Jacqui? She didn't, she told herself. She really didn't.

"If you would please sit down, we'll make you as comfortable as possible and begin."

She complied, sank into another cloud and nearly groaned with delight. She had no idea who made this chair, but she was going to find out and order a dozen, she thought, as once again she drifted off into the twilight.

"Are you ready to wake up?"

Jill heard the question through cotton layers of sleep. The voice was soft, filled with amusement and very, very masculine. The voice was *Colin's*. Jill instantly awoke.

He was sitting beside the cloud chair, holding her

hand and smiling over at her. "I gather the morning has been a relaxing experience for you?"

"It's been okay," she said cautiously. After all, she'd come here under protest, so she didn't want him to be too pleased with himself. "I didn't sleep all that well last night, so I took the opportunity for a cat-nap."

"Good. I'm glad you were able to get some rest. Are you ready for lunch?"

If there was one thing she was dead certain of, it was that she was too relaxed to get dressed and go out to one of the trendy restaurants where the movers and shakers lunched. "No."

His brows arched skeptically. "Don't you want to get your money's worth? It's included in the package price."

"Oh, I hadn't realized."

"Well, now that you have, come on." He gave a light tug on her hand. "After lunch, you've got only one or two more things to do, and then we're out of here."

She was so relaxed she wasn't certain she could have made it out of the chair without his help. When she was finally on her feet, she suddenly remembered that she was naked beneath the terry robe. She adjusted it and tightened the belt. She hadn't been con-scious of her relative nakedness until he had shown up.

He looked down at her and stroked her hair away from her face. "I don't think I've ever seen you this relaxed."

She gave a light chuckle. "I'm sure no one has. They not only relax your muscles here, I think they also relax your bones."

He slid his hands along the sides of her face and tilted it up to his. "Relaxed looks good on you," he said softly, huskily, the glints of gold in his brown eyes holding her gaze until she felt in danger of falling into them.

When he lowered his mouth to hers and lightly brushed his lips back and forth over the full softness of hers, it was almost as if she'd been waiting for it. Suddenly nerve endings sprang to life, carrying tingling warmth to all parts of her body. And the thought fluttered through her mind that he wasn't being fair. She was too relaxed to put up any defense against him. Not that she could remember that a defense had helped her last night when they had danced.

He slowly parted his mouth, and she parted hers in response. Heaven help her, she knew what was coming next, and she wanted it. His tongue delved deeply into her mouth, not with the force he had used last night, but with a leisurely gentleness that had her almost incoherent. Heat bloomed between her legs. Surroundings were forgotten. She could only concentrate on what he was making her feel.

His hand slid inside her robe to cup one bare breast, and his thumb stroked her nipple until a soft moan escaped her. As soon as it did, he pulled away.

Her next breath came hard. Her body had been left aching and hurting. She gazed up at him, confused and unsure. What was he doing to her?

He exhaled a long, shaky breath. His face seemed etched in torment, but his next words erased that idea.

He gestured vaguely. "That's what Des would have done." He took her hand and practically dragged her toward the door. "Come on."

Dazed, she followed him out of the room and down

the hall toward yet another door. "Jacqui has set our lunch up in here so we can have some privacy."

Privacy. Oh, yeah, right, she reflected with numbed sarcasm. That was exactly what they needed.

He opened the door to a brightly lit room awash in greens and peaches. The colors had been translated onto sumptuous fabrics that upholstered the chairs and couches. In one corner, where a green ficus grew tall and lush, there was a table set for two, with their plates and glasses already filled.

She headed for it and the champagne she saw. Without looking at Colin, she chose a chair and lifted the flute to her lips. When she'd emptied it, she looked for the bottle.

A second before she could grab it out of the silver bucket, he got it and refilled her glass. "It might be better if you ate something before you have any more."

The suggestion, though gently made, was received with all the humor of an enraged rhino. Still, she did finally look at her plate. There were large portions of chicken, spinach and fruit salad, along with two small muffins.

With every one of her senses now alive, she realized two things: she was hungry, and she desperately needed to block Colin from her mind.

She picked up the sterling-silver fork and proceeded to attack the food. It was satisfying and delicious.

Her mind was blessedly blank, and amazingly, the relaxation she had gained this morning was still with her. By the time she was finished eating, even her heartbeat had returned to normal and the heat had receded. But she remembered the kiss, the touch—oh, *how* she remembered.

She looked at Colin and saw that he was staring at her. She glanced at his full plate. He must have been watching her the entire time; he hadn't taken so much as one bite of his food. Her gaze returned to him. He was reclining in his chair, his elbow propped on its arm, his face bracketed by his thumb and forefinger.

Carefully she laid her napkin over the arm of her chair. "You said something about one or two more things I had to do?"

He nodded.

"What?"

"A hairstyling and makeup lesson."

"I don't need makeup lessons, but I'll agree to the hairstyling."

"Good." His expression was absolutely enigmatic.

What was he thinking? Did he remember, as she did, how she'd reacted to his kiss? Did he know how his simple touch on her breast had nearly leveled her? Did he know that she felt different from the person she had been the night of her party? And that the difference had started when she awoke the next morning to find that she had slept the night through all tangled up with him?

"And do you have anything planned after the hairstyling?"

He hadn't once shifted position, nor had he dropped his gaze from her. She had the feeling that this was one time when he couldn't figure out what she was thinking. That made two of them.

She looked down at her folded hands and absently noted the clear polish they had applied to her nails as she had slept. It was what she always wore. Her toenails were another matter, though. They had painted them a hot pink. Colin had finally gotten a color on her toenails that made a strong statement.

"We're driving to the airport, where we'll board my plane and fly to the American Virgin Islands."

He paused, obviously expecting her to say something, to object, but instinct told her to remain silent. There could be danger in speaking before she figured out what was bothering her. Besides, she knew there was more to come.

"A friend of mine owns a private island down there that he's agreed to lend us for a few days."

Once again he paused, but she continued to remain quiet. As motionless as she held herself, though, her mind was racing. A private island meant they would be alone, with the possible exception of a staff. Colin and she would basically be alone. For a few days, he had said. Her heart gave a hard thud.

After a moment Colin straightened in his chair. "One of the reasons we're going down there is to give me the opportunity to teach you how to snorkel. Des loves to snorkel." He fidgeted with the edge of his plate, then pushed it away and looked back at her. "So, as I said, we're driving straight from here to the airport. As a matter of fact, our luggage is already in my car. I packed my bags this morning, and while you were busy with your massage and so on, I had Neiman's send over a selection of things you'll need, beachwear and the like, along with suitcases. Jacqui helped me pack the bags and assured me there was everything in them that you'll need. I also called Molly, who drove to your home, collected your medicine, along with a few other things she said you'd want, plus your purse, then brought them over.

They're all packed in a separate case, where you can get to them easily if needed.''

He had thought of everything, and he had taken it on himself to arrange everything behind her back. She knew he expected her to get angry, to tell him in no uncertain terms that she wasn't going anywhere else with him, nor would she let him hijack her aboard his plane. She should. She also knew that, to Colin, she probably appeared eerily calm. She was.

But things were shifting and turning inside her as surely as if they were something tangible she could see on an X ray. She could *feel* them. It was as if she was having her own private, internal earthquake, and it felt every bit as violent as the shifting of tectonic plates. She just wasn't sure yet what the changes were and why they were occurring.

"I promised Molly that you'd call her from the plane so that the two of you can go over anything you need to.''

If she stayed in town, she would throw herself back into her work with her usual intensity, and her questions would be shoved into the back of her mind. She would make sure of that.

Instinctively, though, she knew her questions were too important to go unanswered. Besides, why shouldn't she take a few days off? She'd been working her whole life, starting when she was three years old, when she had begun to work so hard to please a father who could not be pleased.

"Jill?''

She lifted her gaze to him. He looked worried, wary. He wanted an answer. She would give him one. "Fine.''

Seven

Jill stretched slowly awake. Sunshine and a mild breeze glided through a large open door, filling the room with light, the scent of tropical flowers and the soothing sound of the sea's relentless movement. At the door, flowing, sheer, cream-colored curtains blew inward in a slow, undulating motion. It was the same material that was draped over the tall posters of the bed.

The sounds, the scents were all so completely different from what she was used to that for a few minutes she simply lay there, trying to orient herself.

When they had arrived on the island last night, Colin had shown her to this room and set her new pieces of luggage on two matching teak chests at the foot of her large bed. Two smaller bags had gone into the bathroom. He'd also said that when she was ready, there would be a late dinner served on the terrace, but she'd been too tired. Instead, she had showered, rifled through the luggage until she had found a pink silk chemise, crawled into bed and gone straight to sleep.

In retrospect, she supposed the inner turmoil she had endured the past few days had left her exhausted. Even on the trip here, she and Colin had exchanged very few words. She'd taken him at his word and called Molly, issuing instructions as to how to rearrange the rest of her week. Then, instead of going to sit with Colin in the cockpit, she had taken a nice long nap. Even so, she had still arrived on the island feeling exhausted.

She slid out of bed and padded over to the doorway that led out onto a wide stone terrace. Last night, she remembered, Colin had driven them up a hill from the landing strip that he had told her was on the other side of the island from the house. He had said the strip had been carefully constructed so that, no matter where you were on the island, it couldn't be seen, except from the air.

Last night she had been too tired to try to get her bearings. Now, though, she saw that the house did indeed sit on a hill.

She didn't even have to step out onto the terrace to see the deep-green vegetation that carpeted the hill all the way down to a shimmering white beach and the multihued blue sea beyond. Flowers so brightly colored they didn't seem real made enormous bouquets amidst the trees and bushes. She could even see white wicker lounge chairs with several matching small tables placed slightly to the left of her doorway, so that they would be convenient but wouldn't block the view.

She had made a good decision to come here, she

thought. The island was an entirely different world, with a different kind of beauty than what she was used to. If any place could get her out of her normal routine where she lived, slept and ate business, it would be this island. The tranquil beauty would allow her a perfect environment to try to process all that had happened to her in the past few days. Yes, she had definitely made a good decision.

And since she was going to be here for a couple of days, she might as well get dressed and venture out to see what or who she could find.

Colin had said the purpose of the trip was to teach her to snorkel, so she rummaged in the suitcases and found six different two-piece bathing suits with matching cover-ups in an array of colors. She eyed a dark-pink two-piece with a critical eye. Skimpy. Decidedly skimpy. But the other suits didn't look much larger.

With a sigh, she took the bikini and its cover-up into the bathroom and put it on.

Viewing herself in a floor-length mirror, she frowned. The bottom half of the suit started inches below her navel and its legs were cut high. The top was little more than two bra cups held together by string. At the same time, nothing vital was exposed, and it wasn't *completely* outrageous. She twisted around to get another view, and the conclusion she reached surprised her. She looked pretty good in the suit.

She smiled at herself. The very fact that she was here, with two scraps of fabric serving as a swimsuit, was yet another clue that she was changing. What she didn't know, and what she was here to figure out, was whether or not she liked the changes.

Plus, she had never been on a tropical island before, and swimsuits did seem to be called for. She took one more glance at herself in the mirror. How stupid of her. Why did she feel she had to defend herself *to* herself?

The cover-up was a lovely soft drift of pink-flowered material. She slipped it under one arm and tied it at the top of the opposite shoulder. There, she thought with another smile at herself—nothing showed but a shoulder and her arms.

Last night she'd delved into one of the smaller bathroom bags only long enough to find a new toothbrush and a tube of toothpaste. Now she took a longer look in each bag and found the touch of the beauteous Jacqui in the variety of facial creams, cleansers and makeup, all bearing the Jacqui's logo. According to several of her female acquaintances, Jacqui's products were excellent, so okay, she would use them.

She didn't have to look in the other bag. She knew it bore Molly's touch and contained all her medications. Hopefully she wouldn't have to use any of them.

She washed her face, brushed her teeth and slathered one of the creams on her face and neck. Then she turned to the task of her hair and found there wasn't much to do.

The hairstylist who had cut her hair yesterday had layered it. The cut had lightened its weight and revealed the wayward natural curl she had fought all her life to tame. The stylist had also shortened her hair to brush her shoulders and added wispy bangs. As a result, all she had to do was run her fingers through it, wet or dry, and it looked the same as when the stylist had sent her on her way yesterday.

She briefly shook her head at her reflection in the mirror. The haircut was one change she definitely hadn't gotten used to yet. Returning to her bedroom, she donned a pair of sandals she found in one of the suitcases and headed for the terrace.

But after only a few steps, she stopped. Colin was standing at the other end of the terrace, staring out at the turquoise sea, one hand braced against a post, the other hand holding a cup of coffee.

And he was wearing nothing but a pair of dark blue, tight, low-cut swim briefs.

Very brief. Very tight.

She flushed and swallowed with a suddenly dry throat. Seeing him in profile as she was, the bulk of his sex was obvious.

She was riveted by the sight, and her heart began to pound as if it were about to burst out of her chest. But why? She had already felt his size and shape when they had danced. In his arms, on the dance floor, encircled by other couples, she had nearly come apart at the feel of him pressed against her lower body. She still could remember how she had ached for him.

She couldn't allow that to happen here. She wouldn't.

Besides, as she had just told herself, they were on an island where bathing suits were called for. She might as well get accustomed to the sight of his hard body, his sex....

Unbidden, heat flowed into her veins, until her whole body felt feverish.

She barely managed to stop herself from retreating to her bedroom. This was *not* a good way for her to start off her visit here on the island. She had stopped hiding in her bedroom closet a long time ago, and she had no intention of starting now, however metaphorical it would be in this situation.

Slowly she walked toward him, but she forced her gaze away from him and scanned the rest of the terrace. Behind Colin was an outdoor living area, complete with comfortable-looking couches and chairs covered with fabrics that faithfully duplicated the tropical colors around them. There was even a fireplace, and overhead, a ceiling fan turned, as did several others along the terrace.

His gaze was so fixed on the sea, he didn't see her as she approached, which was just as well. No matter how hard she tried, she could no longer avoid looking at him. Closer now, she saw water droplets drying on his muscled body and golden-brown hair.

"Good morning," she said. Hopefully conversation would get her mind off his body.

He turned with an uncomplicated smile of welcome. "Good morning."

His smile warmed her in a way that had nothing to do with sex. Thank *goodness*. "Is it? Morning, I mean? Time-wise, I'm thrown. All I know is that I fell into bed last night, slept the sleep of the dead, and when I awoke, the sun was already up."

"That's pretty much all you need to know. Time really isn't important here in the islands." His gaze skimmed her attire. "You look lovely."

"Thank you," she said, then instinctively tried to deflect his attention away from her. "This island is dazzling."

"I'm glad you like it." His smile told her he knew what she was doing.

Damn it. He was back to reading her mind. "Have you already been for a swim?"

He nodded. "The water was great. You're going to love it."

She glanced toward the sea. "That remains to be seen."

"Right." He reached for a blue-printed T-shirt that matched the blue of his swimsuit, slipped it over his head and down over his chest. Water quickly stained it in the places where he wasn't yet dry, such as his chest, where she'd just seen water droplets glistening. She closed her eyes, as if the act would banish the sight from her mind. It didn't work.

"First things first," he said briskly. "Since you missed dinner last night, I bet you're hungry."

"You'd win that bet," she said, glancing around and seeing a long rectangular table off to the side of the living area. It was set for two.

He took her hand. "Come with me."

It seemed that was all she had been doing for the past three days.

She settled into the chair he held out for her; then he took a chair at a right angle to her. There were several covered dishes already on the table, along with a large fruit centerpiece.

As if on cue, a caramel-colored young beauty with close-cropped black hair glided into view, carrying a white carafe. "Coffee, ma'am?"

"Yes, thank you. Oh, I need decaffeinated, please. Is that a problem?"

"Not at all. That's what this is."

"Jill, this is Liana. Liana, this is my friend Jill."

"Hello," Jill said and received a warm smile in return.

"Welcome to Serenity," Liana said as she poured Jill's coffee.

"Serenity?"

Liana moved to a sideboard, exchanged carafes, then strolled around the table to replenish Colin's cup. "It is the name of our island."

"Liana and her family are caretakers of the island," Colin inserted.

"How nice," Jill said, looking back and forth between the two of them. "I can already see that the island was well named."

Liana and Colin exchanged smiles, and something clutched at Jill's heart. Their smiles were filled with intimate familiarity. Were they involved? Was Liana the woman with whom he had fallen in love? And if so, how had she broken his heart? Obviously they still felt warmly toward each other.

Liana directed her lovely black-eyed gaze on her. "Was there something special you'd like to eat this morning, Ms. Baron?"

"I'm not sure," she said, staring at the island beauty, reflecting that Colin had a way of drawing beautiful women to him. Yesterday it had been Jacqui. Today it was Liana. She gave a soft sigh. What did it matter, anyway? "I am hungry, though."

"Just name your first choice," Colin said. "If we don't have it, you can go on to choice number two."

"All right, then. How about French toast with—" she glanced at the fruit bowl "—kiwi fruit, and crisp bacon on the side?"

"We can do that, ma'am."

"Wonderful." She stared at Liana's warm smile and decided she couldn't blame her if she was in love with Colin. It sometimes seemed as if half the women she knew were. "And please, call me Jill."

"Thank you, Jill. Colin?"

"What she's having sounds good."

"Mama and I will get right on it." Liana turned and disappeared through a doorway.

Just then a gust of wind blew through the covered terrace and ruffled Jill's hair. Instinctively she lifted her face to the breeze.

"You look as if you belong here," Colin murmured.

Slightly embarrassed to be caught in what had been an unguarded moment, she turned the comment back on him. "So do you. You must come here often."

"Why do you say that?"

"Because you and Liana seem to know each other well."

He nodded, eyeing her thoughtfully. "Well, to answer your question, I do come here often—or rather, as often as I can manage. And yes, Liana and I know each other very well."

"How well?" As soon as she said it, she wished for the words back.

Suddenly Colin's eyes began to twinkle. "What have you got going on in that beautiful head of yours? Do you think Liana and I are lovers?"

The sight of gold lights dancing in Colin's eyes was something to behold. She felt a quickening low in her belly. It could mean she was just hungry, but she seriously doubted it. "Are you?"

He shook his head. "No, Jill. I've known Liana and her family for ten years, ever since I started coming here. We're good friends, and that's it. Plus, I don't think her husband would approve." He tilted his head and gazed thoughtfully at her. "Okay?"

She shrugged as if it didn't matter one way or the other. "Sure." She reached for a glass pitcher of orange juice and poured herself some. "So you've been coming here for ten years?"

"Yes."

"The person who owns this island must be a very *good* friend."

"He is."

"*You* own this island, don't you?"

He smiled. "Along with Des."

"I didn't realize you two were so close."

"I told you right from the beginning that we were good friends."

She chewed on her bottom lip. She supposed Colin had done her a great favor by bringing her to an island Des owned half interest in. So why did she feel a sudden panic?

"Why didn't you tell me who owned the island?"

"Because I was afraid if you knew it was partly mine, you might feel trapped in some way."

That was *it*. Her panic had nothing to do with Des and everything to do with Colin. He had her in a place from which she couldn't escape—escape from *him*.

"If at any time you decide you want to leave, just tell me."

She nodded. Once again he had read her mind, which by now she had come to consider almost normal. Maybe it was because he had told her they could leave any time she wanted, but all of a sudden she didn't feel trapped anymore. And strangely, anticipation bubbled through her like champagne. The question was, *what* was she anticipating?

"Are you and Des planning on developing the island?"

"It's as developed as it's likely to get. We love it just as it is, though someday we may build another residence for those times when we both might like to bring our families here at the same time."

She had been about to point out the money they could make if they did decide to develop it, but the thought of Colin with a family constricted her throat to the point that she doubted she could even make a sound.

Colin with a wife and children.

Troubled by the idea, she frowned. But after all, she reasoned, just because he hadn't yet married and started a family, that didn't mean he wouldn't in the future. And the fact that he had even brought up the possibility of building another residence meant that marriage and a family were something he hoped to have.

"While your breakfast settles, I thought I might take you on a mini tour of the island. Or, if you'd rather, we can go straight into the swimming pool."

The hand holding her orange juice halted halfway between the table and her lips. "Swimming pool? There's a swimming pool on the island?"

He nodded. "Within walking distance, though you can't see it until you get there."

"Isn't a pool redundant here?"

He chuckled. "I think so, but Des and I decided to go ahead and put one in. Apparently there are some people who want to be able to see what's under them when they swim at night—therefore, the pool."

"I bet you're not one of those people."

"You're right. The ocean is wonderful at night."

She found herself tangled up in the depths of his eyes. Lord, it was no wonder women fell for him left, right and center. "You mean you're going to teach me how to snorkel in a pool? Colin, *I* have a swimming pool in my own backyard. For that matter, so do you. We could have just stayed home."

"I want to go over the basics in the pool first, so I know you'll be able to handle it out there." He nodded in the direction of the sea. "Once you've got it down, then we'll head for the reef I've got picked out for you."

"Oh." She sipped at her orange juice, then decided to go back to the coffee. "I suppose that's a good idea. But tell me something. From what little I know about snorkeling, it looks relatively easy."

"Once you learn the basics, it is."

"Okay, so I don't see you—or Des, for that matter—being content to merely swim along on the surface of the water. If you two do anything, it would be scuba diving."

His dimple appeared. "You're right, but there are two reasons I decided to bring you down here and teach you how to snorkel. First, you can learn it much faster than you can learn to scuba. And after your first snorkeling trip, it will whet your appetite for scuba diving." He paused and eyed her speculatively. "And if you do convince Des to marry you, that would be something he could teach you."

Once again his answer made sense. But what *didn't* make sense was that she hated the answer.

"By the way, can you swim?"

She couldn't help but laugh. "Do you honestly think I would consider snorkeling if I couldn't?"

"Okay, but how *well* do you swim?"

She thought over his question. "I used to be pretty good, but I haven't been swimming since I was in high school. My father made sure my sisters and I could swim."

"Considering there's an enormous lake at the edge of the Double B, I can see why. He wouldn't have wanted any of you to fall in and accidentally drown."

"I doubt if he would have blinked an eye if one of us had drowned."

"You can't mean that."

"I guarantee you, the day after the funeral, he would be back to business as usual."

"People grieve in different ways, Jill."

"It's not important." She waved the issue aside. "But the reason he made sure we could swim was so that we could race against each other. It was all part of his teaching us to be competitive. It was also the reason he taught us to play golf, tennis, baseball, horseshoes and any other sport he could come up with. It's the reason I stopped swimming as soon as possible, and as a result, truthfully, I'm not sure how far I can swim now."

He stared at her for several moments as if he was contemplating saying something—no doubt something about her father—but then he seemed to change his mind.

"You won't have to worry. You'll be wearing a belt that will keep you buoyant, and a vest if you still don't feel secure, plus the saltwater helps. However, I would never take out someone who didn't know how to swim at all."

"Then why didn't you ask me before now?"

He smiled. "Because if you couldn't swim, I figured I'd just teach you."

"Teach me to swim, huh? As easy as that. You know, you missed your calling. You should have been a teacher."

"You think?"

She nodded. "I'm sure teaching history and mathematics couldn't be that much different from teaching a woman how to accept a man's touch, or teaching her how to dance close to a man, or even teaching her snorkeling. Just another lesson in a long line of them, right?"

He smiled. "Right." He looked up. "Ah, here's our breakfast. Thank you, Liana."

Jill untied the pink wrap and draped it over a lounge chair by the pool. Colin let out a long wolf whistle. "I've got to say that I have excellent taste."

She shrugged, self-conscious. Colin was standing with his hands on his hips, staring at her with open appreciation.

"I did one hell of a job picking out that suit, but then, you've got a great body to show it off."

Annoyingly, unnervingly, his compliment sent heat to every part of her body. "Oh, quit congratulating yourself and let's get on with it."

"Come here."

Irritated more by the way he was making her feel than his words, she pointed to the underwater steps she was standing by. "This is where we go in."

"Not yet. Come here."

The huskiness she heard in his voice caused her irritation to melt away. And just so she didn't do the same, she stiffened her spine and quickly walked to him. She didn't want him to have a chance to study her body too closely, nor did she want the opportunity to do the same to him. As it was, she was having an extremely difficult time keeping her eyes *above* the line where his swim briefs ended.

When she reached him, he grasped her shoulders and turned her around.

"What…?" Suddenly she felt his hands smooth over her back, spreading lotion.

"No one should go anywhere on this island without having sunscreen on, but especially you, with your fair skin."

She tried to reach around to get the bottle. "Okay, but I can put it on myself."

"Not on your back, you can't. This suit exposes too much skin."

"And whose fault is that?"

"The designer's, I suppose."

She rolled her eyes in exasperation, but since he couldn't see her face, the effort was lost on him. Thank heavens, because in the next moment, her exasperation turned to pleasure.

As he rubbed the lotion onto her shoulders, he gave her a light massage. Then he continued slowly downward in a very thorough and sensuous manner. His long fingers didn't miss an inch of her, even slipping beneath the string that held the bikini top around her, slowly sliding toward the sides of her breasts, coming breathtakingly close to the fullness, lingering there, caressing, stroking.

The air blocked up in her lungs. She couldn't breathe. If he reached just a little farther…just a little farther…his fingertips would brush her nipples.

She closed her eyes and felt herself sway. She wanted to ask him to stop but couldn't find the words.

She wanted to walk away, but her legs would not obey.

Now he was below her bra line, to her waist, still caressing here, massaging there. When he reached the line of the suit's bottom, his fingers dipped beneath its edge, not far, but just enough to make her hold her breath.

Then he was on his knees, rubbing oil into her upper thighs, delving beneath the high cut of the suit's legs, then around to the sides of her buttocks.

She reached out for the support of a lounge chair. "I—I can do the rest," she said, though her voice was only a whisper.

Without answering, he simply continued down her legs to her calves and ankles. Then he was in front of her, and she hadn't even seen him move.

She couldn't see. She could only feel his hands stroking lotion on her ankles, her shins, her knees and up. He was using both hands, one on each leg, and the concentration he was giving to the task had to be the same as the concentration Leonardo da Vinci must have brought to the task of painting the *Mona Lisa*.

She cleared her throat. "I really think—"

At the tops of her thighs, his fingers slipped beneath the suit, deep enough to feel the tightly curling hair there.

She gasped.

He stopped, froze, but he didn't move his fingers. His breathing was ragged. He stared at the place where her thighs joined.

Suddenly he stood, took several steps and dived cleanly into the pool. And as his body arced against the blue sky into the crystalline water, she caught a glimpse of his hard, full arousal straining against the material of his swimsuit.

Eight

She faked a headache. As soon as Colin surfaced in the pool, Jill claimed that a sudden, excruciating pain had struck one-half of her head. And all the time she was doing it, she called herself ten different kinds of coward.

But she didn't care. There was no way she could get into the pool with Colin now, be close to him and bear having his hands on her again—not after he had just stroked and rubbed most of her body in an intimate sensual manner that had left her knees weak and her limbs shaking.

What was more, the sight of him as he dived into the water had been proof positive that he had also been affected, though she knew it was in a different way than she.

She understood that men didn't need to feel all the things women did to get sexually excited. All it took for them was the most minor stimuli, which made it all the worse for her. What he could make her feel with a mere twinkle of his eyes meant nothing to him. As for her...she would think about it later.

She grabbed the cover-up, wrapped and tied it around her, then started back up the path to the house. He quickly caught up with her, lifted her into his arms and carried her the last half of the way.

There was no way she could protest. After all, he had helped her through the real thing and was concerned. As soon as she had told him she had a headache, he had surged out of the pool and headed after her. He hadn't even bothered to dry off.

Instinctively, it seemed, she rested her head on his shoulder and wound her arms around his neck. His skin was still wet and slick. She tried not to feel anything, but her effort was doomed. Just the contact of her skin against his was enough to bring back the heat and the memory of his fingers inside her bikini bottom.

Blessedly, Colin walked fast, and soon he was gently laying her on the bed. "What medication do you want?" he whispered.

She closed her eyes. She didn't want to see his concern for her. She didn't want to see the masculine bulge in his swim briefs. Though his arousal had disappeared, no doubt due to his anxiety over her, just the outline of his sex through the spandex was enough to make her mouth water. "Don't bother with it. I'll get up in a minute."

"Just tell me, Jill."

This was going to be tricky. She needed to get rid of him as fast as possible, but based on how he had acted the other night when her pain had been very real, he wasn't going to leave until he was satisfied he had done everything for her that he could. "Bring me the bag."

He did, along with a glass of water. He helped her sit up and opened the bag for her. She picked one of the milder prescriptions, opened the cap and shook one into her hand. "Would you please get me a wash-cloth for my eyes? A cool, wet one?"

He frowned down at her. "Take the pill first."

She had no recourse. She put the pill into her mouth, surreptitiously maneuvered it under her tongue and took a swallow of water. Satisfied, he returned to the bathroom. She had just enough time to replace the pill in its container before he reappeared with the cloth.

"Thank you."

She lay back amidst the pillows and covered her eyes with the cloth.

"What else can I do? Do you want me to close the shutters to make it darker in here?"

"No, I want to feel the breeze. The cloth will keep the light from my eyes." It suddenly hit her that she was talking in complete sentences, even communicating with the proper words. She was lousy at deception, she reflected ruefully, or at least she was when it came to Colin. She hoped he hadn't noticed, but just in case, she slurred her next words. "Leave. I'll sleep."

She felt him sit down on the bed beside her and take her hand. "Are you sure? Last time…"

"Last time I didn't catch—" she took a breath, reminding herself to slow down and slur the words "—the headache in time. This won't be as bad." She gently pulled her hand from his. "All I need is to sleep it off."

"Listen, Jill. There's a clear button on the phone, here on the table to your immediate left. It's within easy reach for you. If you need something, *anything,* all you have to do is push it, okay?"

"Yes…but I won't have to."

She waited, but he didn't move. For a while she thought he was going to stay, as he had the other night. The fact that his concern was genuine made her feel horrible. And strange. Other than Molly, there was no one who worried about her. Yet Colin obviously did. Why? she wondered, and received no answer.

She forced her mind back to the problem at hand— getting rid of him. Little by little she managed to relax and to check her breathing until it was even and slow. Finally he eased off the bed and quietly left by the terrace door.

And at last she was alone, but any coherent line of thought continued to elude her, so, falling into an old habit, she went over the few things she knew for a fact.

She had agreed to come to the island because she had felt it would give her the opportunity to figure out what the changes she was feeling were and why they were happening. She also knew that, so far, she hadn't had the time or the opportunity. Colin had been all-pervasive in both her waking and sleeping hours.

She had the time now, though. Yet the harder she tried, the more confused she became. Her thoughts were too scrambled, too tangled up with sensations and emotions that, in one way or another, all had to do with Colin.

Des, she told herself sternly. *Des. Des.*

She repeated the name over and over in her head, trying to get herself back on track to her original goal.

Three days ago, she had agreed to cancel all her appointments for the next few days. She had even taken the unprecedented step of agreeing to a partnership with Colin to develop their adjoining parcels of land. And she was putting herself through an emotional and physical ringer by taking these lessons from him.

But her problem was, she kept forgetting why she had agreed to Colin's plan in the first place. Everything she had done in the past few days had supposedly been to help her win Des's attention as a woman and not as a stepcousin to whom he had never been particularly close, anyway. Yet all she could think about was Colin.

She took a deep breath. Her brain obviously needed oxygen, although heaven knew, the island had a surplus of fresh air.

She supposed it was inevitable that she hadn't been able to think clearly. If these lessons had taught her nothing else, it was why her female acquaintances lost their heads and hearts to Colin. He was a virile, deeply sexual, wildly attractive man.

And the lessons he was giving her provided a full dose of all those elements. To get her accustomed to a man's touch, he'd had to stroke and caress her. To teach her how to dance with a man, he'd had to demonstrate. She understood. Some things simply couldn't be told. They had to be shown.

But as a result, her mind and body were reacting to Colin, when she was sure that was the last thing he wanted. From his viewpoint, she was sure he saw himself as merely a substitute for Des.

And the changes she felt inside her? Maybe it was as simple as the fact that Colin's lessons were working—that in some indecipherable way they were making her softer, more open to loving a man.

Des. Of course she had meant that Colin's lessons were making her more open to loving *Des.*

She barely managed to stifle a groan. The answers she had come up with all made perfect sense, yet for some unfathomable reason, she couldn't accept them.

The afternoon wore on. Hard as it was to believe that she might still be sleep deprived, she actually managed to doze on and off. But even with the cloth over her eyes, she was always aware when Colin came to check on her. He would stand at the end of the bed, watch her for a few minutes, then leave again.

By five o'clock, she was bored. Her faked headache had accomplished what she had hoped. It had enabled her to regain her equilibrium and put what was happening to her into a context. If she couldn't accept the explanation one hundred percent, at least it made sense. Sort of.

Plus, if she tried to analyze what was going on with her any more than she already had, she would get a *real* headache. She wasn't used to inactivity, and there was a paradise right outside her door.

She got up and went in search of Colin. She now felt strong enough for that snorkeling lesson.

On the terrace, just outside the open doors of the house's enormous main room, their dinner had been served on a round table. Surrounded by freshly picked red hibiscus, a candle burned in the center of the table. Soft, romantic music floated in the air around them. Small white lights in cleverly placed, hollowed-out spaces of the terrace had come alive. Exotic night-blooming flowers perfumed the gentle breeze. A full moon laid a shimmering silver path across the now dark sea.

Jill had never been given to flights of fancy, but she could truly say that tonight had an almost magical quality about it.

To top it off, Colin sat across from her, looking like every woman's dream of a man, dressed with casual elegance in an open-necked, light-green silk shirt and tailored tan slacks.

They had finished their dinner, and Liana had cleared the table. When she had inquired if there was anything else they would like, Jill had decided on a glass of champagne, instead of dessert, and Colin had ordered a cognac.

After Liana had served them their drinks, she said good-night. Colin had told Jill that Liana and her family lived in a compound of homes built on a private section of the island that offered them their own beach.

Which meant that she and Colin were now completely alone.

Jill sat back and took another sip of her champagne, aware that she was experiencing yet another new feeling—contentment. It wouldn't last of course, but while it did, she planned to savor it. "You know, if you and Des could somehow bottle up nights like this one and sell them, you could each make a fortune. Or perhaps I should say *another* fortune."

Colin's dimple appeared as he gave her a lazy

smile. "I know what you mean. Nights like this are just one of the many reasons I've come to love this island so much."

"I can see why. I've always loved dawn, not only because of the colors of sunrise, but because the sight of it offers the promise of a fresh new day. But with nights like this, I could change my mind."

"Ah, but you haven't yet seen one of our dawns."

She nodded. "I plan to do that very thing in the morning. I'm looking forward to our snorkeling trip."

"I'm really glad. There's unbelievable beauty beneath the sea. The place I've chosen for your first snorkeling trip tomorrow is extraordinary. The reef has grown up to around fifteen to twenty feet below the surface in that area, and you'll easily be able to see it all."

Anticipation rippled through her at the idea. "How are we going to get there?"

"By boat."

"I can't wait."

He grinned wryly. "Even though you haven't yet entirely mastered the art of clearing the snorkel tube?"

She shook her head. "I still don't understand how you expected me to do that. When the tube fills with water, what good is blowing three times in quick succession?"

"That's how you clear out the water."

"Uh-uh. Not if the water comes in at the exact same time you've breathed out and your lungs are empty."

He laughed. "That's why I wanted you to practice in the pool today. At least now you're familiar with what to expect once we're in the sea tomorrow."

She grinned. "It's just a shame that you don't have a glass-bottom boat."

He tilted his head, looking at her with an amused expression. "Oh, come on. You're not going to let a little water in your snorkel scare you off, are you?"

"No way."

"That's my girl. All you need is a little more experience and it will start to come naturally. You'll see."

Her pulse quickened. He'd called her his girl. Naturally it was just one of those casual phrases that people throw out on occasion. She wasn't even sure he knew he had said it. But she did.

Yet more changes in her. Four days ago, if someone had told her she would actually be looking forward to a snorkeling trip, she would have told them they were crazy. And if a man had called her his girl, she would have verbally cut him off at the knees. But now… "I'm not overly concerned. If the snorkel fills with water, or if I forget to breathe through my mouth, instead of through my nose, I'll simply lift my head out of the water."

"And I'll be right there beside you in case you get into any serious trouble."

She nodded.

This afternoon, in the pool, he had given her his instructions without once unnecessarily touching her. She had solved the problem of having him apply sunscreen to her by borrowing one of his T-shirts to cover her. Then she had been able to easily apply the sunscreen to the rest of her body.

And if her heart had given an occasional thud at what she had perceived to be a heated look in his eyes or an expression of desire on his face, it was simply because her body hadn't caught up with her mind's new rational line of thought.

"Have I told you how beautiful you look tonight?"

Her heart gave another thud. At this rate, she reflected ruefully, she might want to consider having a thorough cardiological exam when she returned home.

"Thank you."

She had chosen a long, cool sundress made of silk-lined voile in blues and greens. It had been the colors that had made her reach for it earlier this evening, plus its modest neckline, along with a skirt that consisted of separate pieces that tended to drift outward when she walked. Small straps spanned her shoulders, then crisscrossed her back to about three inches above her waist.

Since the bodice was lined, she hadn't felt the need to wear a bra, which made the dress even more comfortable. Yet one more sign of change in her. Their "date" at the Midnight Blues Club had been the first time she had ever gone outside her home without a bra. Then, she remembered, she had felt naked. Tonight she hadn't thought twice about it.

Everything was happening so fast it was no wonder she was having trouble catching her breath and thinking straight.

"Has anyone ever told you that you have a wonderful instinct for women's clothing?"

His eyes began to twinkle, and a funny fluttering started in her stomach.

"No, and coming from you, that's quite a compliment. As I've said before, you have impeccable taste."

She gazed down at her champagne flute, picked it

up and put it back down again an inch from where it had been. "Have you ever invited another woman down here before?"

"No."

"Have you ever done anything similar with another woman—similar, I mean, to the lessons you're giving me?"

"No."

Those two answers drew a smile from her. "Not even trying to get a woman to wear a softer look?"

He laughed. "And don't forget the part about showing more skin."

"Believe me, I couldn't."

He shook his head. "I don't think you can say anything I've bought you would fall into the risqué category." He paused, considering. "Sexy, maybe, but not risqué."

She had never thought of herself as sexy until Colin had come along and given her his undivided attention. With his lessons, with the clothes he had chosen for her, but most particularly in the way he looked at her and treated her, he had made her feel aware of being a woman in every sense of the word.

It sounded like such a simple and natural way to think, but not in her case. She had never before thought of herself as a woman with her own individual sexuality, much less with the ability to feel at least partially comfortable with it. It was as if Colin had removed an obstacle and given her a completely new outlook.

She took a sip of champagne. "You know, in retrospect, I realize I've probably made these lessons difficult for you. For one thing, I was more set in my ways than I thought. And I also realize now that you were right about my approach to men. It was extremely...businesslike.''

He chuckled. ''You must be feeling very mellow tonight to admit to all that.''

She laughed. ''I must be. I think it's a combination of the night and the champagne.''

''Then I'll simply have to order up more nights like this one, along with cases and cases of champagne.''

His statement had sounded as if he, *personally,* had liked the results of the combination, and heat quickened through her body. *Stop it,* she ordered herself. More than likely he had meant he would order the combination on Des's behalf.

His expression turned serious. ''I'm just thankful you caught that headache in time. I wasn't sure whether or not you'd even be able to have dinner tonight.''

She hated the knowledge of her deception, but she refused to let herself break eye contact.

He tilted his head in that thoughtful way of his to which she was becoming accustomed. ''You know, I don't think I've ever seen you as relaxed as you are right now, or even heard you laugh as you did a minute ago. No matter what comes out of this trip, it will have been worth it to have seen you this way.''

''No matter what comes out of this trip? You mean if I don't get Des?''

He shrugged off her question. ''There's just one thing missing.'' He plucked one of the red hibiscus blossoms from the centerpiece, leaned across the table and slipped it behind her ear. Sitting back in his chair, he studied her. ''Perfect,'' he whispered.

Warmth shimmered throughout her. She had to

clear her throat before she spoke again. "You know something else I've just realized about you?"

"I can't even begin to imagine."

"You're a very patient man."

He gazed at her for a moment with an expression so enigmatic she didn't even try to decipher it. Finally he said, "I suppose I am."

"And there's something else I've realized. I don't know that much about you. I mean, you and I have traveled in more or less the same group for two years now, yet I don't know even the most basic facts about you."

A slow smile appeared on his face. "That's very good, Jill."

"What is?"

"You've just arrived at another very important lesson, and all on your own, too."

"What are you talking about?"

"The lesson we haven't gotten to yet. The lesson that teaches you the need to show interest in the man you are trying to attract."

"I'm not just *showing* interest in you, Colin," she said with real annoyance. "I really *am* interested."

"Even better. So, okay, what would you like to know? I'm pretty much an open book."

In the blink of an eye, her annoyance vanished. She grinned teasingly. "Oh, yeah? I'm not sure I believe that about you."

"Try me."

His soft, husky voice drifted over to her on a wave of the music and sent warmth skimming down her spine. "Well, okay—as I said, basic stuff. For instance, where were you two years ago before we met?

No, wait—let's start even farther back than that. Where are you from?''

"A small town in East Texas you've probably never heard of.''

"You may be right, though I do own land in East Texas.''

"I know, but in a different part.''

She had gotten past the stage of being surprised that he knew more about her that she did about him. "Do your parents still live there?''

"I wish they did, but no. My mother died when I was twenty-nine. My dad died just a few years ago.''

She needed to respond, but since grief over the loss of a parent was foreign to her, she had to fall back on a cliché. "I'm sorry. Do you have any other family still there?''

"An aunt and three cousins.''

"And are you close to them?''

He nodded. "We make it a point to get together every so often.''

It was funny, but she had never thought of Colin as having a family, roots or ties. Perhaps it was the way he had seemed to appear out of nowhere two years ago. And to hear that he was still close to his remaining family also vaguely surprised her.

Her father had never fostered closeness between her and her sisters—just the opposite, in fact. Since Tess had married, she was making an effort to change that. So far, though, Jill had managed to avoid most of Tess's family gatherings. As for the ever elusive Kit, Tess was going to have to catch her first.

"Tell me more about your parents. What did they do?''

"My mom was a homemaker. She took care of my

dad and me, grew her own vegetables and canned them. And once she even won a blue ribbon at the state fair for her peach pie.''

Her eyes widened. ''You've *got* to be making that up.''

He burst out laughing. ''Why do you say that?''

''Because *no one* has a mother like that.''

''Sorry, but I did. She was wonderful. I still miss her.''

Colin was a sophisticated, urbane man, yet he was telling her that he had been raised in a small town by a mother he had obviously adored and fed food she had grown herself. It didn't seem real, but then, most people would probably say the same about her own upbringing.

''What did your father do?''

''He owned a general store. He wasn't setting the world on fire with it, mind you, but the income was sufficient for the three of us, and that was all that mattered to him.''

''Oh, I get it now. You grew up in Mayberry, right? Your aunt's name is Bea, and Andy Griffiths was the sheriff, with a deputy named Barney and a son named Opie.''

He chuckled. ''Sorry to disappoint you, but no. My parents were good, simple people who raised me with a great deal of love and taught me, by example, the difference between right and wrong. It was a marvelous life for a little boy, but as I grew older, I also learned that life can be difficult, too.''

''What happened?''

''When I was ten years old, my father lost everything.''

''You mean his store?''

"His store, our home and most of our belongings. He even had to sell our good car and buy a junker that ran only half the time. And it all happened because Dad trusted the man who kept the books and paid the bills for the store, along with our personal bills. Unfortunately, that trust was grossly misplaced."

"But why did your dad trust this man so much? Surely there were signs, something that should have clued him in early on?"

"There probably were, but you see, Dad's education had stopped in the eighth grade because he had to drop out of school. His father had died, and he had to go to work to help his mother. Believe it or not, it's a common enough story when you live in the country deep in East Texas. At any rate, by the time Dad realized something was wrong, it was too late. The man had bled Dad and the store dry, and Dad had no savings to fall back on."

She sat forward. "But the man was caught, right?"

"Yeah, but by that time he had already spent the money. He was put in prison, but justice didn't do Mom and Dad any good. The people to whom Dad owed money went to court to force Dad to liquidate."

"It must have been awful for your parents."

He nodded. "It was. Yet in one way, it was good."

"How can you say that?"

"Because by watching how my parents handled their problems, I was taught invaluable life lessons, things I probably would never have learned in any other way."

"I'm not sure I understand. How did they handle them?"

"With great pride and dignity. We rented one of

the smallest, shabbiest houses in town, but my parents never showed any sign of being ashamed of their reduced state. And because they didn't, I didn't, either. In fact, I never once saw anything to be ashamed of. They hadn't changed. They were still the same loving people who provided me with the same stable upbringing they always had.''

"But how? I mean, how did they cope? How did they put food on the table and buy all the things they needed, not to mention things a growing boy needs?''

"Mom planted a new vegetable garden, but she planted three times as much as she had before, so that she could sell the extra to the neighbors. And she started buying my clothes from the town's thrift shop. At any one time I probably had only two pairs of jeans and three shirts that fit, but Mom made sure they were clean and neatly ironed. She also took in other people's ironing.

"As I became more and more aware of what was going on, I became even prouder of my parents. If anything, the love they gave me grew stronger, as did their love for each other. Many nights after I went to bed, I could hear my mom waiting up for my dad to come home so that she could serve him a hot meal. And I saw her rub his shoulders and back at night when he'd done so much physical labor his whole body would be screaming with pain.

"But through it all, Dad very calmly, and with great perseverance, went about working to get his store back. He worked two jobs, sometimes three, but he never complained, and he never once wavered in his determination. Eventually his patience and hard work won, and he was able to buy back his store.''

Completely fascinated, Jill had been hanging on his every word. "That's an *incredible* story, Colin."

"My parents were incredible people."

"Obviously. I would have liked to meet them."

"Why?"

"Because they made you the man you are today."

He stared at her, his eyes dark. Then, slowly, a smile formed on his face. "Careful. You're very close to giving me a compliment."

She grinned. "You don't need a compliment from me. I've never known a more confident person, and now I know where that confidence comes from. You watched your parents handle the worst and successfully come out on the other side, and that taught you that you could do the same."

"Yes, except losing material things is not the worst thing that can happen to you. Losing someone you love is."

"Of course." His answer momentarily flustered her, because she hadn't expected it. As quickly as she could, she went on, "Now I also know why you're such a patient man. Like your father, you're willing to wait and work for what you want."

"So now you know everything there is to know about me."

Not even close, she thought. She might have learned certain things about his background, but it was very clear to her that he kept a great many things on the inside, just as she did. "I have another question. How did you get from the boy who had two pairs of jeans to the man you are today, a self-made man with enough money to buy anything he wants?"

"With dignity and pride, I hope. As soon as I was old enough, I got a job, but no matter how tired my dad became, he wouldn't let me work so many hours that I neglected my schoolwork. He didn't want me to ever find myself in the position he had. He told me to let him take care of Mom and me and of getting back the store. My job was to concentrate on school. That concentration earned me a scholarship. I don't think I ever saw Mom or Dad prouder than they were the day they saw me graduate from college, not even when Dad got back his store or I began to make really big money.''

''I can imagine.'' And she could, just from the tone of his voice. ''So what did you do after graduation? Go to Dallas?''

''Yeah. For the first eight years or so, I lived there full-time. I set quietly to work and began making contacts. Soon one deal followed another and, not so inconsequentially, my first million was followed by more.''

''Eight years is a fairly short time to make that much money. You make it sound so easy, but I know it couldn't have been.''

''No, but don't forget, I learned early on all about hard work and patience. And by the way, I also met Des my first year in Dallas.'' He paused. ''I'll always be grateful for those eight years.''

''Why?''

''Because everything I was able to accomplish during those years gave me the opportunity to shower my parents with things they had never had before— a luxury car, a really nice home, furniture, vacations.'' He shook his head. ''They'd never even been on a vacation before, and they still wouldn't have gone unless I hadn't packed them up and taken them.''

She chuckled. "Much like you did me, you mean?"

He smiled softly. "Yeah. In fact, as soon as the first part of the main house here on Serenity was built, I got to bring them here. They loved it. I was also able to arrange their finances so that Dad never had to work another day in his life if he didn't want to, though he did. I also had the opportunity to tell them how proud I was of them and to thank them for all they had done for me." He paused. "That's really the thing I'll always be *most* grateful for."

A lump formed in her throat. She had no reference for understanding his gratitude to have been able to do those things for his parents.

"But then my mother died unexpectedly. Naturally Dad was devastated, so I returned home and began to run my business out of the back of his store with computers, modems and faxes. Whenever I sensed Dad was doing okay, I'd make overnight trips to Dallas. But by then his health wasn't good, and there was no way I was going to leave him alone for long. He refused to stop working, so to ease some of his burden, I helped him in the store and tried to make it look as if I wasn't doing much."

The memory drew another smile from him. "And while I was at it, I continued to use the money I had made up until then to make more. But when Dad's health began to seriously fail, I became his main caretaker."

"But why? You had the money to hire someone to take care of him."

He looked at her. "Taking care of him wasn't a chore or an obligation for me. It was something I felt privileged to do, though I used my money to make him as comfortable as I possibly could in other ways." He reached for his cognac and took a sip. "And that's the long version of why I only appeared on the social scene a couple of years ago. Before then, I had other priorities."

She sat there for a moment, attempting to absorb all that he had told her. "You know, you may have had the patience, plus everything else you learned from your dad, to help you accomplish what you have, but you also have a rare brilliance."

He shook his head. "Not brilliance."

"No, it's true. Since I became aware of you, I've seen evidence of your work. And you were smart enough to go into exactly the right business. As a venture capitalist, you used other people's money to make money of your own."

"But no client of mine ever lost a cent."

She smiled. "Don't I know it. In some circles, your name is whispered with reverence."

"Funny. That's how I've heard your name mentioned, too."

She laughed. "Oh, sure you have."

"You should do that more often."

"What?"

"Laugh." He stood, reached for her hand and pulled her to her feet. "That's enough of the past. For now, let's concentrate on the present."

"How?"

"By dancing."

Nine

Like the night, their dance felt magic to Jill.

Colin moved them slowly around the terrace in a way that was as romantic as the music that filled the air. He held her lightly, one hand at her waist, the other hand holding hers out to the side.

The dance was as different from the way they had danced at the blues club as sunlight was to moonlight. Their first dance had been rawly sexual and darkly dangerous. This was more like a dream, soft and sensual.

At times they simply swayed together; at other times they did a slow, graceful waltz. But always, always, their bodies were in tune. She didn't even have to think to follow him. It was as natural as breathing, as sweet as the flower-scented night, as inevitable as the tides.

She wasn't even aware of her feet touching the

ground. She was floating, the lightweight panels of her skirt drifting outward like undulating ribbons of silk. She was intoxicated, not on champagne, but on the night, the music and most of all Colin, yet she felt no alarm.

Her gaze was locked with his, because there was nothing else she wanted to see. And when his steps became even slower and he drew her even closer, she decided there was nowhere else she would rather be than held tightly in his arms. Her body recognized his, softened and melted into his.

She drew her hand from his, slid it around his neck and up into his hair. His hands joined at her back, and his fingers delved beneath the dress's straps to her bare skin.

The heat started gradually, winding its way through her veins. Her nipples hardened against the silk fabric; her breasts began to ache and swell. She had experienced the same things many times over the past few days, but this time she had no urge to try to censure her feelings. Then the heat reached the spot between her legs and flared. She would have fallen if he hadn't been holding her so firmly.

The solid ridge of his arousal pushed against her lower body. Physically Colin wanted her, but intellectually, emotionally, she was sure he didn't. After all, to him they had made a business bargain, a bargain, moreover, that involved one of his best friends.

But it didn't matter to her, not tonight, not at this moment. Since the beginning, there had been a sexual tension between the two of them that couldn't be denied. Every time he had touched her, he had made her entire body pulsate with desire for him. His kisses had left her decimated to the point that nerves and needs had continuously warred inside her.

And it had all left her confused, her thoughts and feelings twisted and tangled to the point that she hadn't known what was happening to her or what it all meant. She still didn't. But now, suddenly, she was tired of trying to figure it out. Most of all, however, she was tired of fighting her feelings.

Just this once, she wanted to make love with Colin. And she wanted to do it now, on this magic night, while the trade winds blew over them.

She pulled herself out of his arms and looked up at him. In his eyes she could see the same heat that she felt inside her. She had seen that same heat before. She had also witnessed his control and the way he could pull himself back from the precipice without taking that one tiny step too far that would have them both falling over the edge and into full-scale passion.

So this time, before he had time to think of all the reasons they should rein in their feelings and say good-night, she grasped his hand and wordlessly began to draw him toward her door.

With each step she took, she expected him to pull her to a halt, but miraculously it didn't happen. She wondered what he was thinking, feeling, but she wouldn't let herself look back at him. She didn't want to chance seeing doubt or wariness or any other negative emotion. Not tonight, when she knew so clearly what she wanted. She continued to her room, through the doors and to the side of her bed.

Liana or her mother had already turned down the covers and turned on the nightstand lamp. A small bowl of freshly cut hibiscus that matched the one in her hair sat beneath it. The lamp's pale golden light lit a portion of the bed. The only other light came from the spill of moonlight through the open doors.

It was more than enough. If she had been blind, she would still have been able to sense Colin if he had been anywhere in the room. His presence disturbed the molecules of the otherwise peaceful atmosphere, threatening to set it on fire; his body heat reached out and wrapped around her; his musky male scent invaded her every pore.

She released his hand, and still without looking at him, she reached behind her back to unzip her dress.

His hand closed over hers and the zipper tab. "Look at me, Jill."

She didn't want to. She didn't want to see his calm visage or hear his rational words.

"*Look* at me," he said, this time his voice hoarse with emotion.

She exhaled a trembling breath. Reluctantly she turned and gazed up at him. His eyes were darker than she had ever seen them, and his face was tight, the muscles in his neck rigid. "Are you sure?"

She could hardly believe it. He wasn't telling her he didn't want to make love to her. Instead, he was thinking of her, leaving the decision up to her without trying to influence her more than he already had.

"Oh, yes." Her eyes moistened with emotion; her words sounded barely above a whisper. "I'm very sure."

He didn't ask another question or give her a chance to say another word. Before she knew it, he had unzipped her dress and pulled it down her body. She stepped out of it, and at the same time her trembling fingers attempted to unbutton his shirt. He pushed her hand aside and quickly did the job.

''Get in bed.''

His intensity and desire were suddenly coming at her in pounding waves, and it dawned on her just how much control he had actually been exerting the past few days.

She kicked off her shoes and did as he said. Once on the bed, she used her feet to push the covers down to the end, then lifted her hips and slipped off her panties.

Colin came down to her, naked and with every muscle in his body hard. He eased himself on top of her, opening her legs with his, then positioning himself.

Her heart hammered with excitement and anticipation, so hard it felt as if her ribs might break. Somewhere in the back of her mind, she knew there were bound to be consequences for stealing these moments out of time with Colin and for taking what she wanted, what they *both* wanted. But she had never felt like this before and probably never would again. And for this one time, this one night, if there was a piper to pay, she gladly would.

''Colin.'' It was a whisper. It was a scream. She wasn't certain which, because above all it was a demand.

His mouth crushed hers, and his tongue thrust deep. She wrapped her arms around his neck, then slid her palms down his back, relishing the feel of the rippling muscles beneath his bare skin that, before now, she had only seen. He closed a hand over her breast and roughly kneaded her flesh, taking her beyond reason and into the realm of heat, haze and animalistic urges and cravings.

She moved restlessly beneath him, her hands covering every inch of him she could reach. She had never been to this place before, where she had absolutely no control over her body, nor did she want any. The kisses and touches had taken her close. The dancing at the blues club, along with the application of the sunscreen, had brought her even closer. But none of them had brought her to the point where she was now.

To be kissed without restraint and touched in a wild urgency of need was incredible, amazing, wonderful. But she wanted more. She wanted Colin inside her so badly and with such violence that if someone had happened to walk in the door and tried to interrupt them, she would have been beyond caring.

And she wasn't afraid. If she had learned nothing else on this island, she had learned that letting herself go was okay and that, no matter what happened, Colin would keep her safe.

She made a sound of frustration and arched against him, convinced she would shatter if she couldn't have him soon. She turned her head, tearing her mouth from his, but she didn't have time to say anything.

"I should go slower," he muttered harshly. "I've wanted this so…"

He entered her with one violent push and buried his thick, long length completely inside her. She caught her breath as sharp, exquisite pleasure jolted through her. Then again. And again. And again.

And then she didn't have time to consciously breathe anymore. He began to slam into her, time after time, and with such ferocity that the bed shook and her body was jarred. But she met his every thrust with her own, lifting her hips to take him more deeply into her. She felt possessed, like a wild woman who couldn't get enough of him.

She was on fire. Her blood was boiling. Her nerve endings were being scraped with a hot, soothing, stimulating, liquid ecstasy. He entwined his hands with hers and pressed them back on either side of her head. She looked up at him and saw that his eyes were almost black, his expression pure male aggression.

She had never known she would love the powerful, sexual mastery of a man. She had never even known such rapture could exist between a man and a woman. She wasn't even sure what was coming next, but she could feel her body readying.

Unbearable, sweet, hot pressure was building inside her. She tightened her grip on his hands and, with tears streaming down her face, bucked beneath him. He bent his head and drove his tongue deeply and roughly into her mouth, taking her there in the exact same fast, exhilarating, jackhammer rhythm he was using to drive into her.

Suddenly overpowering sensations gripped her. She arched her upper back off the bed and came apart, climaxing with a loud cry as she was carried away on waves of pleasure so large, so intense and so incredible, she could only go with them. Seconds later, Colin's entire body stiffened and he followed her as a deep, hoarse growl came up out of his being, carrying the sound of her name with it.

He had blown it.

Colin cradled Jill against him with her head resting on his shoulder. Tenderly he brushed tendrils of damp, dark hair away from her face. Her eyes were closed, and she was as still and limp as a rag doll.

As for himself, his heartbeat had yet to return to normal.

What was he going to do now?

The plan had been to get her away from her everyday life and pressures, so that here on the island, with its slower way of living, she would have very little to focus on but him. In this environment, he had hoped she would relax and get to know him as a person, rather than as someone to banter with at parties or, conversely, ignore.

Well, she had certainly gotten to know him, he thought grimly. The problem was, things had happened out of order.

His first objective, actually his *only* objective, had been to make her fall in love with him.

He had never thought it would happen over these few days. But he had thought, hoped—God he'd *prayed*—it would give him, at the very least, a niche in her life and, at most, a solid foundation on which the two of them could build a deep and lasting relationship.

He loved her. He had known it since the day he had figured out why he had initially been so attracted to her. She didn't know it, but her scars and his were the same. And her wants and his were also the same.

She had never had a family, not in the real sense of the word, and though she might not consciously consider that a loss, the scars had been there that night for him to see, to recognize, to feel. And he had seen something else, too. Deep down, in a part of her soul that she had done her best to seal off long ago, when she had lost her mother and her father had taken over her raising, she wanted one.

He, on the other hand, had had a family—no one could have had a better one—but he had lost them. And ever since, he had wanted a new one, one of his own making. But until that night, when for an instant something had opened up inside her that had allowed him to see into her soul, he hadn't known with whom he wanted to make that family.

But because of what had just happened between them, they both could be doomed never to have one, at least, not the kind they both wanted. He was convinced they could only have that with each other. For once in his life, though, he hadn't been patient. During the past few days, despite his best intentions, he had rushed and overwhelmed her.

She moved against him; her hand slipped onto his chest, and he felt his loins stir. Closing his eyes, he gritted his teeth. He could take her again, right now, but making love to her a second time would only compound his error—or much worse, since he doubted he would be able to stop at twice.

He had purposely set out to make the night a romantic one, including the dance. But as the dance had continued, he had instinctively drawn her closer. When it came to her, he had so little willpower it scared him to death.

And when she had pulled away, taken his hand and drawn him into her bedroom, his brain had started to shut down. Saying no to her would have been a near impossibility. He didn't even know where he had gotten the strength to ask if that was what she really wanted. But when she had said yes, it would have taken the end of the world to stop him from taking her.

Still, he had been too rough, too quick. Their first time should have been different, yet looking back on it, he didn't know how it could have been. Quite simply, he had been starved for her.

How was he going to turn things back around when he still wanted her so badly he was in danger of exploding?

She moved, rubbing her cheek on his shoulder, and one leg found its way over his.

"Jill?" he murmured, despite himself, kissing the top of her head.

"Mmm?" Her foot flexed and rubbed against his shin. Her hand slid through the curls of his chest hair over to his nipple.

He groaned and put his hand over hers to still it. "Are you all right?"

"Uh-huh."

Beneath his hand, her fingers slid back and forth over his nipple. This time he firmly clasped her hand and rolled over on top of her. Her hair lay in a tousled mass around her head; her lips were red and swollen, her lids half-closed, her eyes drowsy with sensual lethargy.

"I better warn you," he said, his teeth gritted, his control held by a slender thread, "you keep that up and I'll be so deep inside you again, so fast and so hard, you won't know what hit you."

She slid her hand up the side of his face and parted her legs. "I'll know."

Without another word he drew his buttocks back and once again drove into her, hard, fast and without mercy. A powerful, white-hot passion held him in its grip. Sanity had been stripped from him. Beneath him, willing and hot, she writhed and strained. He slammed into her time and again, taking them both higher and higher, then clung to her as he soared with her to a pinnacle of ecstasy he had never known before.

After that, he knew there was no way he could stop. He might have only this one night with her to last the rest of his life, and he planned to make the most of it. Actually, there was nothing else he could do. He was like an addict who had gotten a taste of a drug and now couldn't do without it.

The next time he pulled her to him and entered her, he extended the lovemaking as long as he could bear. By now, he knew just how sensitive she was and that, at times, he only had to touch her in a certain way to make her climax.

Gently, slowly, he stroked in and out of her pulsating velvet flesh. At the same time, he stroked his hand up and down her side, stopping occasionally to tweak her nipple and lightly massage her breast. Soon she was trembling and clawing at his back for completion. Then he slowly withdrew from her and rested his hard sex on her lower abdomen.

It was torture for him, but it was the sweetest kind, watching her face react to everything he did. He spent a lot of time nibbling at her nipple, pulling it into his mouth, then scraping his tongue back and forth across it until she softly cried and said his name over and over. Then he switched to the other.

In the next moment Jill did something he hadn't even considered. She took control, reached for him, shifted, and just like that he was inside her again. She arched and writhed against him, high and hard. He lost his control, his mind, pounding into her until seconds later he felt the tight squeezing of her inner contractions. And as she bowed her upper back off the bed, he heard the soft, wild cry he had come to love. Then he exploded into her and everything faded to black.

The dawn was everything she had expected it to be, Jill reflected, standing in the doorway of her bedroom, watching the blues and roses shift across the sky, the dark waters of the sea gradually lighten to purple and indigo. Just for a moment she allowed herself the luxury of lifting her face to the morning trade winds. They wound their way through her hair, wet from a shower, and moved over her freshly moisturized skin.

She threw a quick glance over her shoulder at Colin. He was still sleeping. Under any other circumstances, she probably would be, too. This morning, however, she had too much on her mind.

She had known what she was doing last night when she had taken his hand. Every bit of what had followed had been her fault. She had told herself that she wanted to make love to Colin just once, and she had. She should have been satisfied with that once, but she hadn't been. She had been greedy, hungry, and had practically made him continue.

Granted, it hadn't taken much encouragement, but then, he was a man, and as she had noted before, if a woman shows herself to be willing, a man doesn't need any more motivation. But to give Colin his due, up to that point, he had shown remarkable restraint, considering the job he had set out to do.

No, it was her fault. She didn't regret it, but she

also couldn't be more embarrassed about it. If there was a way she could get off this island by herself before he awoke, she probably would. As it was, she didn't know how she was going to meet his eyes.

And the ultimate irony? She had come to the island to give herself time to figure out all the changes that were happening inside her. At one point yesterday, she thought she had figured it out. But after last night, she was more confused than she had been when she arrived.

Making love to Colin had shaken her world apart, and she wasn't certain it could ever be put back together again—at least, not in the way it had been.

"What are you doing up so early?"

Her heart gave a hard thud at the sound of his sleepy voice. Would there ever come a day when her heart wouldn't react in that way to him? Would there ever come a night when she could look across a crowded room without wanting him?

"You were right," she said, without turning to look at him.

"About what?" He sounded irritated, grumpy, not fully awake yet.

"The dawn. It's spectacular."

She heard his heavy exhalation of breath, then movement, as if he was rearranging pillows.

"What are you doing up, Jill? You can't have gotten enough rest. And why the hell are you dressed?"

After her shower, she had slipped on the pair of slacks and plain white T-shirt she had worn on the flight here. "I think it's time I left. You can stay if you like, and I'll hire a charter from one of the bigger islands."

Behind her, he swore, then more movement. Her

blood started racing as she realized he was getting out of bed.

"Jill…"

He was coming toward her. She stepped out onto the terrace and glanced in the direction of the other end. "The table is already made up, and there's a carafe of coffee out. I think I'll go have a cup while you dress."

"Jill, come back. We need to talk."

She turned and looked at him. He was standing in the doorway, a sheet wrapped around his waist. His hair was a complete mess, more so than usual, and his face sported a night's growth of beard. His eyes were even red and blurry. Yet she didn't think she had ever seen him look as devastatingly handsome as he did right then. "I don't think so." Quickly she walked away.

Showered, shaved and dressed, Colin joined Jill on the terrace. Without looking at him, she broke apart a croissant. "Liana and her mother are wonderful. They didn't really expect us to be up this early, but they had these ready just the same."

"I don't want you to leave, Jill."

Carefully she spread guava jelly on the croissant. "I know I haven't had my final snorkeling lesson, but after my lesson in the pool, I'm sure I could manage in the sea if I decide I'd like to do more of it."

"I couldn't care less about the snorkeling. Let's talk about the real reason you want to leave—what happened last night."

"Last night has nothing to do with why I want to leave." She had never known she could be such a good liar. She had never known her heart could hurt this much without breaking. "And there's really nothing more that we need to talk about. You've done a great job with all the lessons, but—"

His head jerked back as if she'd hit him. "If you think for one minute last night was about those damn lessons, you're dead wrong."

"It doesn't matter."

"It happens to matter a *hell* of a lot."

"Then, no, Colin, I don't believe last night was about the lessons. It was just about two people on a beautiful island, surrounded by a beautiful night, who had been in close proximity to each other for several days. Something was bound to happen and it did. But now it's over and I need to get back to Texas."

Silence stretched between them. Jill could feel his gaze on her, almost hear him thinking. She just wished she knew *what* he was thinking.

She had known it was going to be difficult to get him to forget last night, especially since she herself would like nothing more than to go back to bed with him right now and not get up for another week. But she couldn't betray what she was feeling by even so much as a flicker of an eyelash. She needed to get away from him, and she was running out of ammunition.

"Okay," he finally said. "We can leave today if you want, but not before we talk."

"Do you happen to know where Des is today?"

Colin froze. Color leeched from his face. His gaze filled with black rage. His chair scraped back and he stood. "He's at the Double B visiting his father. We'll leave in thirty minutes. Be ready."

Ten

Using one foot, Jill slowly pushed herself back and forth in the swing that hung in the gazebo. A soft breeze filtered to her through a screen of junipers. Somewhere she heard a bird call. In a distant meadow, cattle grazed.

She was in the backyard of the Uvalde farm where her sister Tess and brother-in-law, Nick, were spending their summer. In fact, no matter what the season, they would hop on a plane and come here every chance they got.

And after three days here, Jill had to admit, the place did have a certain charm. It also had a peace and warmth about it that she had badly needed.

Not too far away, Tess bent to cut yet another iris from her garden to go into her already full basket of flowers. When she straightened, she looked over at Jill. "I'm going to put these in the house and bring us out some iced tea," she called. "Does that sound good to you?"

"Great," Jill called back.

Three days ago, acting on an instinct she still didn't entirely understand, she had contacted her sister from Colin's plane and asked if she could come and stay with them for a short while. Tess's yes had been full of enthusiasm. And now, seeing how happy Tess was that she was there, Jill felt guilty for all the times she had rebuffed her.

Her mind returned to Colin and their flight back to Dallas. He had broken his silence only once, by calling her on the intercom to ask if she wanted him to arrange a charter for her to take her to the Double B. She had declined, saying that she had already called Molly and asked her to make the arrangements. What she hadn't told him was that she had no intention of flying to the family ranch to see Des.

Hearing the screen door slam, she glanced up to see Tess, dressed in shorts and a brief top, strolling toward her with an iced tea in each hand. When she reached her, she handed her one, then sat down beside her.

"I like your farm, Tess."

"Thank you. Nick and I both love it. Strictly speaking, though, it belongs to Nick's family—well, actually his grandmother—but Nick and I are the only two who actually want to make it our second home. Nick's sister and her family know they are always welcome, and we try to have as many gatherings as we can. As a matter of fact, since Nick's grandfather died, his grandmother Alma usually comes and stays for a few days when we're here, and it makes us all so happy. During the winter, we fly in for as many three-day weekends as we can.''

Jill nodded. ''Like I said, nice. Good tea, too, by the way.''

''The mint came from the garden.''

Jill chuckled. ''It's been hard for me to accept that you actually *like* to garden. I mean, you never have before. It was something we were never exposed to.''

Tess nodded pensively. ''I know, but the difference is, this is a real home, something I'd never known. Before I married Nick, I had my place in Dallas, but it wasn't a home, not really. I was always traveling or working.'' She shook her head at the memory of her past. ''Now Nick and I also have our Austin home. I still work and travel, though I try to limit the latter as much as possible. And Nick has his own work. But no matter which home we're at, it's filled with love and the memories we're making with every moment we spend together. I've learned *that's* what makes a home. And—'' she grinned ''—we're hoping very soon now to start turning a room in all three homes into a nursery.''

''Nursery?'' Jill asked, shocked. ''Is this an announcement?''

''I *wish*, but no, not yet. Soon, though. I can feel it'll be soon.''

''That's wonderful,'' Jill murmured sincerely. ''I'm very happy for you and Nick.''

''Okay,'' Tess said, her tone suddenly brisk and businesslike, ''that's enough about me. It's time to tell me what's going on with you. When you arrived here, you looked pale as a ghost—in fact, almost sick. Since then, you haven't said much except for superficial conversation, but I'm relieved to say that you do look a little better."

"I'm sorry. I know I haven't been very good company."

"I'm not complaining. I just want to know what happened to bring you here now, at this particular time, when you've turned down countless other invitations. And while you're explaining, I also want to know what you're running from."

Jill studied her sister. Tess's blond hair was pulled back into a ponytail and tied with a wrinkled ribbon that couldn't quite manage to hold the myriad escaped tendrils. Her face positively glowed. "You know what? I've never seen you look more beautiful or happier. Love obviously suits you."

Surprise crossed Tess's face. "You're calling *me* beautiful, when you're the acknowledged beauty in the family? Now I know the answer to my questions—you're obviously sick."

Jill's lips curved in wry amusement. "It's true, you know. You've always been beautiful, but now…" She let her words trail off, and her gaze drifted away from her sister toward the garden. "Instinct brought me here. As for what I'm running from…I guess I have to say Colin."

Tess frowned. "Colin? Colin Wynne?"

Jill nodded, then proceeded to fill her sister in on the bargain she and Colin had struck—and its outcome. She finished with, "So once again I'm confused. When I arrived here, I knew only one thing for sure. I'm in *lust* with Colin."

Her sister choked on a gulp of iced tea.

With a glance at her to make sure she was all right, Jill continued, "But since I've been here, I've watched you and Nick. Tess—'' she turned to face her sister ''—there have been times when you and Nick have been sitting across the room from each other, and one of you will smile at the other, and I can actually *feel* the love you have for each other. Actually, that's very likely what brought me here in the first place—an instinct that you and Nick have the real thing. I wanted to learn about it.''

''Our love?''

Jill nodded again. ''To start with, the love I've seen between you two has simply confirmed a decision I made before I left the island. I don't want to marry Des. He doesn't love me and I certainly don't love him. When I decided to try to learn how to go about getting him, I was convinced that we could have a marriage that would work for both of us on some level, even though I doubted we would actually love each other. I now know just how wrong I was.''

''Deciding you didn't want to marry Des must have been the equivalent of an intellectual earthquake for you,'' Tess said, impressed, ''but I've got to say, I'm very glad you came to that conclusion before it was too late. Which brings us back to Colin.''

''Colin.'' Jill shook her head. ''I'm pretty sure he hates me now.''

''Why?''

''Because he wanted me to stay on the island and talk about our night together. But I knew I couldn't do that without revealing what I felt for him, so I gave him the impression that as soon as we landed in Dallas, I was going to the ranch to use all the lessons he'd taught me to catch Des.''

''But why should that upset him? It's the reason he

gave you the lessons in the first place. That doesn't make sense.''

"I know.'' She gnawed on her bottom lip for a moment. "The only thing I can think of is that maybe he believes I'm going to renege on our bargain. I won't, though."

Tess fished out a mint leaf from her tea and nibbled thoughtfully on it. "There *is* another possibility.''

"What?''

"He loves you.''

Jill shook her head. "There's no way. When we parted at the Dallas-Fort Worth airport, he was ice-cold with anger."

"Do you care?"

"Yeah, I do. Tess, he's a *remarkable* man. On the island, I learned about his background, and it made me feel so humble.''

"Why?''

"Because he's accomplished so much, yet started out with so little.'' She paused. "He also made me feel incredibly sad that I never knew the kind of parental love he had."

"I understand, because for a little bit, I felt the same way about Nick."

"You did?''

Tess nodded. "And you know what conclusion I reached? You, Kit and I are the only people in the world who really know that our so-called privileged life was actually a nightmare. And we each had to learn in our own way how to survive, how to make it through our childhood to become functioning adults. Our father even robbed us of each other's comfort. Nick and Colin may not have had the material things that we had, or the money we inherited to start out like we did, but they had something a lot better. They were able to grow up knowing that, no matter what they did, they were loved unconditionally. If you look at it like that, they started out way ahead of us.''

''I guess that's true,'' Jill said slowly, trying to assimilate what her sister had just said.

''Oh, it definitely is. So don't ever feel humble again, Jill. We've *more* than earned our inheritance, plus we've each taken our portions of the company and skyrocketed them to a success and prosperity our father never even dreamed of.''

''You're *right*.''

Tess grinned. ''Of course I am. So let's get back to Colin.''

Jill sighed. ''As I told you, I have a bad case of lust for him.''

Tess's grin broadened. ''Let me give you a little sisterly advice. Great sex is nothing to be sneezed at.''

Jill tentatively returned her sister's grin. ''I learned that. But, Tess, this is what I want to know. How do you tell the difference between love and lust? I mean, you must have faced the same thing with Nick. How did you decide it was more than lust, that in fact it was true love?''

Tess leaned over and set her glass on the gazebo floor beside the swing, then straightened and reached for Jill's hand. Jill was so startled she nearly jerked her hand away, but Tess merely tightened her hold.

''Listen to me, Jill. You, Kit and I were never taught anything about love, because our father never showed us any. So when it came to figuring out if I loved Nick or not, I didn't have a clue. But in my case, I had some help. Uncle William flat out told me

I loved Nick. And believe me, when I realized he was right, no one was more surprised than I was."

Jill's brows drew together. "So as soon as Uncle William told you that you loved Nick, you instantly knew he was right?"

Tess nodded. "Because as soon as he said it, I started getting these flashbacks of things that had happened during the relatively short time I had known Nick. And I finally understood that it wasn't anything big that had happened between us that should have clued me in to the fact that I loved him, but a series of little things."

"Such as?" Jill leaned toward her, paying close attention.

Tess smiled softly as she remembered. "There was the way that with just a smile he could make me go weak at the knees. The way I practically melted into him when we danced on the night of my birthday."

Jill gasped, but Tess went on, "The easy way he could make me want him. The way I had turned down Des's offer to come rescue me when Nick kidnapped me and brought me here. It all added up. I just hadn't connected love with the way I felt about him, because I didn't know how it felt to love a man—or anyone, for that matter."

Jill stared at her, her eyes wide with shock. "Tess, everything you just said—I can apply every *one* of those things to what has happened between Colin and me, right down to and including how he makes me feel."

"Plus the fact that you are no longer interested in marrying Des."

Jill sat back. "Oh, my God, Tess. *I'm in love with Colin.*"

Tess laughed with pure delight. "Then we've got to get you back to Dallas as soon as possible. And at our very next board meeting, we simply have to address buying our own corporate jets. We spend a fortune on charters."

Tears of happiness spilled down Jill's face, and for the first time in their entire lives, the two sisters hugged.

Jill deliberately arrived late at the charity function. She handed her invitation to the attendant at the door of the large ballroom, then nervously slipped to the side and along the wall, until she had a good view of the front portion of the room. As she had hoped, dinner was over and people were busy milling about, visiting or dancing, but she couldn't see Colin.

The overhead lights were off. Most of the room's illumination came from the glowing flames of the six-inch candles clustered in the center of each round table. In addition, a ceiling had been formed from strings of cleverly intertwined, tiny white lights backed by a cobalt-blue fabric, so that it looked as if thousands of night stars sparkled overhead.

She chewed on her bottom lip, thankful for the coverage provided by the room's atmospheric lighting, along with the preoccupied people. She didn't want to be noticed just yet. As a matter of fact, if she could have had her way, no one would see her but Colin. But she had determined that meeting him for the first time in five days at this event would be the best way to convince him that she loved him. The thought that she might be wrong tightened the myriad knots already present in her stomach.

Molly had doubled-checked the RSVP list, and unless Colin had changed his mind between the time he had accepted and now, he should be here. Gnawing on her bottom lip, she slowly made her way farther down the wall toward the back of the room.

The dress she had chosen for her task tonight was far more daring than anything he had chosen for her, though she had purchased it from the same store where he had gotten the hot-pink dress she had worn to the blues club.

This dress was made of a remarkable liquid-silver fabric that appeared to have been poured over her body. Its cowl neckline dipped dangerously to just above her nipples. In the back, the line of the cowl continued down past her waist and stopped right above the dimples of her bottom. To help her move, the skirt was slit up one side. The dress took its shape entirely from her body, and there was no way the dress could accommodate any underwear, though heaven knows she had tried.

She doubted she would have even had the nerve to wear the dress out of the house if it hadn't been for the matching shawl, lined with an icy aqua silk. Currently it was draped to cover her breasts, with one long end tossed over her shoulder to fall down the middle of her very bare back.

Suddenly she saw Colin, and her heart began its now all-too-familiar thudding. He was as devastatingly good-looking and charismatic as ever in a black tuxedo, one hand slipped with casual elegance into his trouser pocket, the other holding a drink.

He was facing her, with three women arranged in a semicircle in front of him, and he was laughing at something one of them had said. But she could tell his laughter was only a facade. She wouldn't have been able to realize that before their time on the island, but she could now.

Watching him, she turned hot, then cold, then hot again. Lord, could she do this? Her palms were clammy. Her heart was pounding so hard she was sure the fast rhythmic movement was visible through her skin. And if even one more physical symptom struck her, she reflected with a mixture of amusement and terror, she would probably have to seek medical help.

But she wouldn't allow herself to take the easy way out and confront him later in a more casual environment. She drew a deep breath and called on every ounce of courage she could muster. She had a formidable job ahead of her.

With a small prayer, she unwrapped the shawl from around her, turning it into a mere accessory, instead of a cover-up, by draping it over her forearms and letting it fall down the back to beneath her hips.

She started toward him and knew the moment he saw her.

He stiffened, and his smile vanished. Curious, the three women turned to see what or who had caught his attention, and as she neared, it was their greetings that helped alleviate his conspicuous wall of silence.

"Jill, we were wondering if you were going to make it tonight."

"You look wonderful. The new way you're wearing your hair is very becoming."

"My *word,* that dress is gorgeous, though not your usual style at all. What's happened? You must have gotten a complete makeover somewhere."

Still as stone, Colin trained his icy stare on her.

She could now completely understand and empathize with Billie Holiday's lament of unrequited love.

Refusing to be intimidated, she stared right back at him. "Actually, yes, I did—with Colin's help."

"Really?" As if choreographed, all three women looked from her to Colin and then back to her.

She nodded. "Even to the point of buying me clothes. He thought I was dressing too primly and decided I needed to wear more revealing clothes."

"Softer." The one word sounded as if it were strangling him. "And I never bought you *that* dress."

One of the women looked at Colin. "Do you mind me asking why you were, uh, making over Jill?"

He didn't answer, continuing to glare at her, so *she* answered. "It was a business bargain we made, wasn't it, Colin? And as most business deals are, this one is private. However, I will tell you that part of the deal involved lessons."

Ravenous curiosity now etched the faces of the three women.

"Lessons?" one of them ventured.

Jill nodded. "Actually, the lessons could best be summed up with the phrase, *how to torture Jill.*"

With a soft curse, Colin grabbed her hand. "Will you ladies please excuse us?"

With open mouths, the three women nodded in unison.

Tightly gripping her hand, Colin strode toward the rear of the room and the exit, but that didn't fit into her plans. Not yet. Besides, now that the three women were out of the picture, his control had slipped enough for her to see he was practically foaming at the mouth with anger. It would be safer for her to stay within sight of people.

She wrenched her hand from his and stubbornly

halted. He had no choice but to stop and look back at her.

"I'd like to dance," she said.

"What gave you the impression I *care* what you'd like to do?"

He made a grab for her hand again, but she slipped away to an empty space at the back edge of the dance floor, bordering an area close to a wall that held only tall plants and offered a certain degree of privacy. When she turned around, he was there, and she offered up a grateful prayer that he had followed her.

"What in hell is holding that dress up?" he asked, his voice as sharp as razor blades, his eyes as dark as midnight.

With a smile, she moved into his body and slid her arms around his neck. "Willpower," she whispered into his ear.

He yanked her arms from his neck and pushed her away. "I don't know what kind of game you're playing, unless you've got some demented idea of trying to make Des jealous, but it isn't going to work. He's not here."

She shrugged, and the action lifted one breast until the top edge of her nipple's rose-colored areola appeared. His gaze followed the movement, and she saw him swallow hard. "I didn't expect him to be."

His hands clenched into fists at his sides. "Where have you been for the last five days? I know you weren't at the Double B, because I called Des."

"Really? Why were you looking for me?"

"Because…" He stopped and briefly closed his eyes. He must have suddenly realized how he appeared—tensed, almost white with fury, as if he was about to strike her.

He roughly pulled her to him, though not close enough that her body was touching his. "Because," he said in a lower voice, "I called Des to tell him to expect you."

"How thoughtful, but not at all necessary."

A vein throbbed at his temple. "And then I called to make sure you'd arrived safely."

She shrugged again. "I never said I was going to the ranch."

"The hell you didn't. You told me you'd called Molly to arrange a charter for you."

"That's right. To Uvalde. I decided to spend a few days visiting Tess and Nick."

"You...?" His teeth clamped together.

"It's a good band, isn't it?" They were playing a blend of oldies and newer songs, and at the moment a romantic ballad that Elvis had once recorded, "And I Love You So." She doubted Colin was even hearing it. She reached up, slid her arms around his neck and began to dance, moving against him to the song, though he remained still.

"What are you doing?"

She pressed her body closer to him and whispered into his ear, "If I remember correctly, Lesson Number Three. Dance very close to your partner, so that if you want to carry on a conversation, you can press your mouth to his ear." She waited a beat and received no response. "Am I doing it right?"

A growl rumbled up from his chest, and he slid his hand down her spine, encountering nothing but perfumed skin. He yanked one of her arms from around his neck, so that he could hold her hand out from their body. "It's more conventional for *two* people to participate in a dance."

"More fun, too."

His face tightened until he looked like a violent storm cloud about to burst. "Okay, I'm only going to ask you once more, Jill. What are you doing? And do *not* say dancing or attending a party. You know exactly what I mean, so tell me."

Once again she put her mouth to his ear. "I'm putting into practice what you taught me. Lesson Number One was dressing in a softer style and showing more flesh. I believe I accomplished that tonight, don't you?"

Almost involuntarily, it seemed, his hand slipped past her waist down to the edge of her gown, then, just for a moment, he allowed his fingers to dip beneath the fabric to caress one round buttock. He jerked his hand back as if he'd touched fire.

"Damn it to *hell,* Jill. You're not wearing any underwear."

"The outline of any kind of undergarment would have shown through and ruined the line of the dress. You taught me that, remember?"

He uttered a low, violent string of oaths.

If he was suffering, so was she, Jill reflected ruefully. Being in his arms again, inhaling his musky scent, feeling his hands on her—it brought back all the needs and desires she had felt for him that last night on the island. Even now, heat was crawling through her veins and gathering between her legs. But there was no way she could stop now. "Lesson Number Two was allowing your date to help you in and out of the car, which obviously isn't applicable for tonight. And..."

"Never mind."

The band switched to "Layla," one of the most

passionate love songs in the history of rock and roll, playing a bluesy version that was close to the same tempo as the song they had danced to in the club. In every way, the song couldn't have been more appropriate.

The dress and her lack of panties prohibited her from spreading her legs and straddling his as she had done that night, though Lord knew she was burning to. But the famous melody and words, combined with the heavy, sensual beat, compelled her to move her pelvis back and forth against his.

He gripped her shoulders, attempting to hold her away from him. "Don't *do* that."

"Why?" she asked, continuing. She needed the contact. She needed to feel the familiar hard ridge of his sex against her. She needed something to stop the nearly unbearable hot achiness building inside her. "It's what we did at the blues club."

"That was different."

"How?"

"Damn you, Jill." He tightened his grip on her and pushed her away. *"Stop it."*

She glanced around, but everyone was engaged in other activities, and no one seemed overly curious about the two of them, though heaven knew how they could miss what was going on. She could no longer control her breathing. She wasn't sure she would be able to control herself at all if she didn't get some relief from the way she was feeling. But she forced herself to remember why she was doing this in the first place.

"What's the matter, Colin? You can dish it out, but you can't take it?"

He shook his head as if trying to clear his mind.

Abruptly he wrapped his fingers around her wrist, dislodging the shawl from that arm, and pulled her out the exit door and down the hall. The end of her silver-and-aqua shawl trailed on the floor after them.

He shoved her into a deserted service corridor and up against a wall, pinning her there by holding each of her wrists on either side of her head. "Why are you practicing the lessons I gave you on *me* when it's *Des* you want?" His voice was raw; his hands on her wrists were trembling.

She wrested her wrists free, planted her hands flat against his chest and pushed him a step away to give herself some breathing room. "*First* of all, I don't want Des. Not anymore. And *secondly,* I wanted to find out if what you taught me would be good enough to make a man forget a woman he's been in love with for a long while."

"You wanted…?" He looked thunderstruck.

"Well, *is* it, Colin? Can I, using your lessons, cure you of her? Can I make you forget her?"

His brows drew together. *"Who?"*

She lifted her chin. "The woman you're in love with. The woman who broke your heart. The woman who doesn't return your love. The woman you told me about at the blues club," she prompted, wondering why he wasn't getting what she was saying. "You asked me if I had ever loved a man the way Billie Holiday was singing about, so I asked you the same thing."

"Right," he said, slowly nodding, obviously remembering now. "And I said *maybe.* I said *maybe,* Jill. I didn't say *yes.*"

"But it made so much sense. I mean, I've watched women throw themselves at you for the past two years, yet you've remained politely but firmly unattached. When you said 'maybe,' I decided the reason was because you were already in love with a woman, and that she had either broken your heart by turning you down—which, by the way, I can't imagine—or that she was nearby, but for some reason she wasn't in love with you.''

''You got all of that out of my *maybe?* And then for some reason decided to see if you could make me fall out of love with her?''

She nodded, watching him carefully. He still seemed astounded, yet his anger was fading.

''Why, Jill? As an experiment? Just to see if the lessons really worked? Or for the kick of it?''

''No,'' she said slowly, knowing she was about to leap off a cliff with no assurances about where she would land. The old Jill would never have even contemplated such a leap. The new Jill, with her heart bursting with love, did it. ''Because I realized when I was at Tess's that I have totally and completely fallen quite madly in love with you.''

For several long moments, it didn't seem as if he breathed. Finally he drew a deep breath and slowly exhaled it. Golden lights began to glitter in his eyes. ''Okay, well, here's the answer to your question. You can't cure me of my love for the woman I've been in love with for the last two years. No one can.'' With his hand he tilted her face back up to him and smiled tenderly down at her. ''Because it's *you,* Jill. I'm totally and completely in love with *you—quite madly,* as a matter of fact.''

She looked at him in disbelief. Her heart gave the expectant thud, then soared. Colin brought his mouth down on hers, kissing her with the same ferocity with which he had kissed her on the island, and as his tongue drove deeply into her mouth, his hands moved up and down her spine, then dipped beneath the low back of the dress to cup and grip her firm, round bottom. Clinging to him, she became lost—in time, in place, but most of all in him.

Colin drove them to her home as fast as was possible. Inside, on the bed, he pushed the dress off her shoulders and down to her waist, and she lifted her hips to pull it the rest of the way off. Impatiently and with shaking hands, he undressed. Then she was straddling him, sliding downward until he was completely sheathed inside her body. An exquisite pleasure immediately flooded through her, engulfing her, making her shudder, making her moan.

She felt free at last. She no longer had to censor what she felt. She never would again. Loving Colin had given her the freedom of feelings at long last released.

They made love slowly, exquisitely, and completely, their love for each other spilling over into their actions. Every second, every sound, every sensation, was savored. Every caress and every touch was cherished. Until finally, they climaxed together and the world crashed around them.

Later, as she lay beside him, he ran his hand over her still-trembling body. "I've been half out of my mind with worry about you. Molly wouldn't tell me where you were."

"That was my fault, not hers. I needed the time to try to figure out some things."

"Next time you need time like that, *tell* me, okay?"

"Okay, although it won't happen again. Everything is finally crystal clear to me."

"Thank God." He reached for her hand and kissed it. "So when did you decide to give up on trying to get Des?"

"Almost as soon as you started those damn lessons. I couldn't keep my mind on Des. In fact, after that first night at the blues club— No, it started even sooner than that. It started the morning I woke up and discovered I had slept the night through in your arms. I couldn't get that intimacy out of my mind, or your scent, or the way you looked in those briefs. Then you proceeded to send one shock after another at me." She lightly laughed. "There were times when, if you had said 'Des,' I would have said 'Des who?'"

"Lord, I wish I had known. It would have saved me a lot of agony."

"And if *I* had known, it would have saved me the same torture. But you gave me no sign—" she paused and thought "—other than what I thought was normal for a man in close proximity with a woman."

He groaned, and she lightly hit him. "You have to understand, I didn't know a lot about men other than in business. I also didn't know about love." She gave an embarrassed little shrug. "The way I was raised—"

Two fingers quickly covered her lips. "You don't have to tell me. I know. Des, remember? He said your dad kept you girls on such a regimented schedule that you rarely saw him or his father, which might have given you at least a glimpse of kindness and love." His lips curved. "Except he did mention something about William's housekeeper sneaking you a cake on your birthday."

"Yeah, that was pretty much it."

"That was cruelty, plain and simple. From what I've heard, your father was a monster."

She sighed, then rolled over until her head was resting on his shoulder, her hand lying lightly on his chest and her leg thrown over his. "No more. That's all in the past. From this moment forward, we can make the future what we want it to be."

A shudder wracked his body, and he pressed a kiss to her forehead. "One thing. What about your ambition to gain control of the company?"

She fell silent for several moments, and when she at last spoke, her voice was soft. "You have to understand—for so long, my part of the company was all I had. And because of the competitive way we were raised, it was natural for me to want control. But it's simply not important to me anymore, not in any way. And you know, during the last couple of days, when I thought about it, I realized that my sisters and I have never disagreed on anything major concerning the company, anyway. For all our competitiveness, our bottom line has always been what's best for the company." She shifted so that she could look up at him. "Thanks to you, I have so much more now. I've learned what true happiness really is. It's all about loving and being loved."

He bent his head and gently kissed her. "You can't even imagine how happy I am at this moment."

"Yes, I can, because I feel the very same way."

He smiled down at her, then let his head fall back to the pillow. "So tell me about this future of ours. Do you have any specifics in mind regarding what you want?

"Yes," she said slowly, thoughtfully. "I want to

love you and be loved in return, every single moment of the rest of our lives. I want to make our houses into real homes, homes that will not only make us feel comfortable and safe, but be a sanctuary, a retreat from the rest of the world. And I want babies—lots of happy babies who will be so loved they'll never have to think that they have to prove themselves to us.''

His hand moved caressingly over her arm. ''Anything else?''

''Yes. There'll be a garden in every one of our homes where irises from Tess's garden will grow and our children will play.''

''Anything else?''

''I want you to take me to East Texas so that I can see where you grew up and meet your family.''

''Anything else?'' Amusement was creeping into his voice.

She looked up at him. ''I'll want to continue to work of course. But I won't eat, sleep and drink it as I have in the past. For that, I'll have you.''

His smile broadened, and he tightened his hold on her waist. ''Anything else?''

She lightly laughed. ''That's all I can think of for now.''

''What? Nothing else? Are you sure? In my opinion, you've forgotten one very important thing.''

Her brow creased as she tried to figure out what it could be. ''What?''

''Doesn't marriage figure into your wishes anywhere?''

She sat straight up. ''Oh, my goodness, *yes*.'' She looked back at him. ''*Yes*. But—''

He pulled her back down to him. ''No buts.''

She struggled to breathe, because suddenly he was holding her so tightly, but she managed a grin. "I guess I sort of took that for granted. But now that I think about it, I guess I should ask if that's what you want, too."

He gave a loud shout of laughter. "Honey, I've waited for you for over two years. The whole point of working with you on the land development deal in the first place was to give us an excuse to be together. And the whole point of the lessons was to get you to fall in love with me. You're *never* going to get away from me now."

He had called her honey. Contentment flooded through her, and with a secret smile, she snuggled against him. "Just think of all the fun we have ahead of us, teaching each other new lessons."

He rolled over on top of her and slipped into her. "Let's start with a lesson about trying to learn to get enough of each other."

She closed her eyes and gasped with pleasure as he pushed deeper and deeper into her, until he couldn't go any farther. "I'm positive that's one lesson we'll be trying to learn for the rest of our lives."

* * * * *

Look for THE BARONS OF TEXAS: KIT, coming in Fall, 2000, only from Silhouette Desire.

If you enjoyed what you just read,
then we've got an offer you can't resist!

Take 2 bestselling
love stories FREE!
Plus get a FREE surprise gift!

Clip this page and mail it to Silhouette Reader Service™

IN U.S.A.	IN CANADA
3010 Walden Ave.	P.O. Box 609
P.O. Box 1867	Fort Erie, Ontario
Buffalo, N.Y. 14240-1867	L2A 5X3

YES! Please send me 2 free Silhouette Desire® novels and my free surprise gift. Then send me 6 brand-new novels every month, which I will receive months before they're available in stores. In the U.S.A., bill me at the bargain price of $3.34 plus 25¢ delivery per book and applicable sales tax, if any*. In Canada, bill me at the bargain price of $3.74 plus 25¢ delivery per book and applicable taxes**. That's the complete price and a savings of at least 10% off the cover prices—what a great deal! I understand that accepting the 2 free books and gift places me under no obligation ever to buy any books. I can always return a shipment and cancel at any time. Even if I never buy another book from Silhouette, the 2 free books and gift are mine to keep forever. So why not take us up on our invitation. You'll be glad you did!

225 SEN C222
326 SEN C223

Name	(PLEASE PRINT)	
Address	Apt.#	
City	State/Prov.	Zip/Postal Code

* Terms and prices subject to change without notice. Sales tax applicable in N.Y.
** Canadian residents will be charged applicable provincial taxes and GST.
   All orders subject to approval. Offer limited to one per household.
   ® are registered trademarks of Harlequin Enterprises Limited.

DES00   ©1998 Harlequin Enterprises Limited

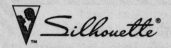

SILHOUETTE'S 20TH ANNIVERSARY CONTEST
OFFICIAL RULES
NO PURCHASE NECESSARY TO ENTER

1. To enter, follow directions published in the offer to which you are responding. Contest begins 1/1/00 and ends on 8/24/00 (the "Promotion Period"). Method of entry may vary. Mailed entries must be postmarked by 8/24/00, and received by 8/31/00.

2. During the Promotion Period, the Contest may be presented via the Internet. Entry via the Internet may be restricted to residents of certain geographic areas that are disclosed on the Web site. To enter via the Internet, if you are a resident of a geographic area in which Internet entry is permissible, follow the directions displayed on-line, including typing your essay of 100 words or fewer telling us "Where In The World Your Love Will Come Alive." On-line entries must be received by 11:59 p.m. Eastern Standard time on 8/24/00. Limit one e-mail entry per person, household and e-mail address per day, per presentation. If you are a resident of a geographic area in which entry via the Internet is permissible, you may, in lieu of submitting an entry on-line, enter by mail, by hand-printing your name, address, telephone number and contest number/name on an 8"x 11" plain piece of paper and telling us in 100 words or fewer "Where In The World Your Love Will Come Alive," and mailing via first-class mail to: Silhouette 20th Anniversary Contest, (in the U.S.) P.O. Box 9069, Buffalo, NY 14269-9069; (In Canada) P.O. Box 637, Fort Erie, Ontario, Canada L2A 5X3. Limit one 8"x 11" mailed entry per person, household and e-mail address per day. On-line and/or 8"x 11" mailed entries received from persons residing in geographic areas in which Internet entry is not permissible will be disqualified. No liability is assumed for lost, late, incomplete, inaccurate, nondelivered or misdirected mail, or misdirected e-mail, for technical, hardware or software failures of any kind, lost or unavailable network connection, or failed, incomplete, garbled or delayed computer transmission or any human error which may occur in the receipt or processing of the entries in the contest.

3. Essays will be judged by a panel of members of the Silhouette editorial and marketing staff based on the following criteria:

    Sincerity (believability, credibility)—50%

    Originality (freshness, creativity)—30%

    Aptness (appropriateness to contest ideas)—20%

    Purchase or acceptance of a product offer does not improve your chances of winning. In the event of a tie, duplicate prizes will be awarded.

4. All entries become the property of Harlequin Enterprises Ltd., and will not be returned. Winner will be determined no later than 10/31/00 and will be notified by mail. Grand Prize winner will be required to sign and return Affidavit of Eligibility within 15 days of receipt of notification. Noncompliance within the time period may result in disqualification and an alternative winner may be selected. All municipal, provincial, federal, state and local laws and regulations apply. Contest open only to residents of the U.S. and Canada who are 18 years of age or older, and is void wherever prohibited by law. Internet entry is restricted solely to residents of those geographical areas in which Internet entry is permissible. Employees of Torstar Corp., their affiliates, agents and members of their immediate families are not eligible. Taxes on the prizes are the sole responsibility of winners. Entry and acceptance of any prize offered constitutes permission to use winner's name, photograph or other likeness for the purposes of advertising, trade and promotion on behalf of Torstar Corp. without further compensation to the winner, unless prohibited by law. Torstar Corp and D.L. Blair, Inc., their parents, affiliates and subsidiaries, are not responsible for errors in printing or electronic presentation of contest or entries. In the event of printing or other errors which may result in unintended prize values or duplication of prizes, all affected contest materials or entries shall be null and void. If for any reason the Internet portion of the contest is not capable of running as planned, including infection by computer virus, bugs, tampering, unauthorized intervention, fraud, technical failures, or any other causes beyond the control of Torstar Corp. which corrupt or affect the administration, secrecy, fairness, integrity or proper conduct of the contest, Torstar Corp. reserves the right, at its sole discretion, to disqualify any individual who tampers with the entry process and to cancel, terminate, modify or suspend the contest or the Internet portion thereof. In the event of a dispute regarding an on-line entry, the entry will be deemed submitted by the authorized holder of the e-mail account submitted at the time of entry. Authorized account holder is defined as the natural person who is assigned to an e-mail address by an Internet access provider, on-line service provider or other organization that is responsible for arranging e-mail address for the domain associated with the submitted e-mail address.

5. Prizes: Grand Prize—a $10,000 vacation to anywhere in the world. Travelers (at least one must be 18 years of age or older) or parent or guardian if one traveler is a minor, must sign and return a Release of Liability prior to departure. Travel must be completed by December 31, 2001, and is subject to space and accommodations availability. Two hundred (200) Second Prizes—a two-book limited edition autographed collector set from one of the Silhouette Anniversary authors: Nora Roberts, Diana Palmer, Linda Howard or Annette Broadrick (value $10.00 each set). All prizes are valued in U.S. dollars.

6. For a list of winners (available after 10/31/00), send a self-addressed, stamped envelope to: Harlequin Silhouette 20th Anniversary Winners, P.O. Box 4200, Blair, NE 68009-4200.

Contest sponsored by Torstar Corp., P.O. Box 9042, Buffalo, NY 14269-9042.

PS20RULES

ENTER FOR
A CHANCE TO WIN*

Silhouette's 20th Anniversary Contest

Tell Us Where in the World
You Would Like *Your* Love To Come Alive...
And We'll Send the Lucky Winner There!

Silhouette wants to take you wherever
your happy ending can come true.

Here's how to enter: Tell us, in 100 words or less,
where you want to go to make your love come alive!

In addition to the grand prize, there will be 200
runner-up prizes, collector's-edition book sets
autographed by one of the Silhouette anniversary
authors: **Nora Roberts, Diana Palmer,
Linda Howard** or **Annette Broadrick**.

DON'T MISS YOUR CHANCE TO WIN!
ENTER NOW! No Purchase Necessary

Silhouette ®
Where love comes alive™

Visit Silhouette at www.eHarlequin.com to enter, starting this summer.

Name:

Address:

City: State/Province:

Zip/Postal Code:

Mail to Harlequin Books: **In the U.S.**: P.O. Box 9069, Buffalo, NY
14269-9069; **In Canada**: P.O. Box 637, Fort Erie, Ontario, L4A 5X3

*No purchase necessary—for contest details send a self-addressed stamped envelope to:
Silhouette's 20th Anniversary Contest, P.O. Box 9069, Buffalo, NY, 14269-9069 (include
contest name on self-addressed envelope). Residents of Washington and Vermont may
omit postage. Open to Cdn. (excluding Quebec) and U.S. residents who are 18 or over.
Void where prohibited. Contest ends August 31, 2000.   PS20CON_R2